The RED FLAG

Julia Maiola

My dearest Mikayla,
thank you for being a great
friend and a great suitemate.
I hope you like the book and
remember, never give up on what
matters you! Always fight!
Love,
[signature]

maiolajulia@gmail.com
@CaptainMaiola

The RED FLAG

NOTE

This is a work of fiction. Names, characters, places, and incidents either are the products of the author's imagination or are used fictitiously. Any resemblance to actual events, locales, organizations, or persons, living or dead, is entirely coincidental.

Cover image by Noupload
Cover design by Julia Maiola

Dedicated to 127 + 1
Your friendship means everything to me

ACKNOWLEDGMENTS

THIS BOOK WAS A JOURNEY that began on February 22, 2013. Luckily, it was not a journey that I had to take alone. Along the way I had a number of people who helped me, guided me, supported me, listened to what may have seemed like nonsense ramblings, and read paragraph after paragraph of text messages.

Firstly, to the girls of Suite 127, Jessica, Samantha, and Mikalya. Not only did you give up your own down time to sit with me and talk about this book, but you also made the past year one of the best in my life. You will never know how grateful I am. Thanks for being there through every step of this project, for all of the advice, and for constantly putting up with my questions and updates.

To Sara, my best friend and library partner. Through the ups and downs you've stuck with me. You've had a large impact on who I've become as a person, and your help with this book has also impacted me as a writer. It means everything. Thanks for reading the first draft and for helping me with Twitter.

To my sister-in-law, Sam. Thank you for all of your editing help and sharing your bookworm enthusiasm with me.

To my parents. I could never thank you both enough for the support and encouragement. It was you who turned me into a writer when I was little, taking me to the library, listening to books on tape in the car, and fostering my creativity and imagination. Just remember, if I ever quit my job to become a full-time author, it will be your fault. Thank you for listening when I needed to talk, and talking when I needed to listen.

To my brothers, Joe and Lucas. You two have always been there for me, no matter when or what the need. You are my superheroes. You then gave me two loving sisters, and now that care has doubled.

To my nephew, Mason. Thanks for reserving your smiles for me.

To my uncle, Angelo. Thank you for being a fan since even before this book was finished. I can only hope that it lives up to your expectations.

To anyone who has pushed me to write better, learn more, and be a better person. Thank you for your inspiration.

Finally, to the readers of this book. It's you who make this possible. Thank you!

The RED FLAG

CHAPTER ONE

S HE COULD STILL HEAR THE SCREAMING. Still smell the blood in the air. Though she had pulled the blankets up to her chin, they did little to comfort her. Her eyes drifted to the starboard side window, just a circle of glass in the wood, where only the starless sky met her. It seemed even the moon, trembling behind the clouds, had abandoned her to this lawless ship.

Her father's voice seemed to call to her in the night, "Alice... Alice!" She lifted her face, only for the voice to hiss and grate back into the deceiving sounds of the ship as it sailed along the American coast. Alice remembered running to her father across the ship, into his open arms.

"You'll be safe," he had promised. "You'll be safe."

And he had pushed her away, urging her to hide. And as she left him she had looked back. Why couldn't what she had seen then be the last? Why couldn't her final image of him be as he was in that moment, his hands at his sides, his soft brown eyes fondly following after her, a brave smile on his lips?

Instead Alice saw him as she had while crouching in her hiding place behind supply barrels. Though her vision had been distorted through tears, her father had been clear enough. He had been kneeling. Kneeling before a tall man wearing a black frock coat. She had heard the deep thuds of the man's boots as he stepped closer to her father, his hand resting on the hilt of a sheathed sword.

And the sword had flashed. A dance of sunshine had momentarily lit up the deck as white light met polished metal, and then bounced off. Almost invisible, the sword had been drawn from the pirate's side and brought to Alice's father's chest, penetrating all the way through to his heart. Alice's father had made a sound that was both startled and strangled. He had lilted sideways, but the sword, still stuck in his chest and still being held by its wielder, had prevented him from completely falling over.

The tall man had tugged on his weapon. When it didn't budge, he had sighed. It had been a sigh of annoyance and boredom. Then he had pulled with some strength and, as the sword slid free, her father had collapsed to the wooden deck beneath him.

Alice had shaken with silent sobs, desperately trying not to make a sound for fear of jeopardizing the secret of her presence. But one sob had escaped. She had quickly put both hands over her mouth and froze.

The tall man had lifted his face away from the man he just killed and had turned it toward her. It had been then that Alice first saw his cold, emotionless eyes. They had been a dark shade of blue, an expanse of deep, dangerous ocean. She had felt the hair on the back of her neck stand up, and goosebumps prickle her arms. She had quickly ducked down out of sight, closed her eyes, and held her breath, waiting for the dreaded footsteps of the man walking toward her. However, she had heard no such sound and realized that he had miraculously not seen her.

When Alice had lifted her head, she had been met with a clear line of sight to her father. He had been staring at her. Right at her. But his eyes, once so full of love, were lifeless. Unseeing. Dead.

Now Alice shivered. She sat up in bed and wrapped a blanket around her shoulders. The memory had already started over again in her head. She stood suddenly. The wood floor of the ship felt rough under her bare feet. She lifted a leg and took a step toward the bedroom door, easing it back down without a sound. Opening the door about an inch, she pressed her eyes to the crack, and gave a peek.

He was sitting at the desk, asleep, his head resting backward against the chair that he occupied. Alice watched him for a while. She noted the way his chest rose and fell with each breath that he took. Right now he looked like any average man. He didn't look like a pirate captain capable of merciless murder. He didn't look like the evil monster that had killed Alice's father in cold blood. Yet he was.

Carefully, Alice closed the door and went back to bed. As much as she feared being grabbed back into that memory, she feared waking the captain more. Much more.

So she stared at the ceiling with wide eyes, felt the pirate ship rock gently. Felt it closing in around her. Crushing her.

And the captain in the next room, she imagined that she could hear his breathing. Imagined that his breath was somehow suffocating her like a poison. The ten year old remained in this state of mind for the rest of the night.

CHAPTER TWO

TWO DAYS EARLIER

LICE WANDERED ABOUT THE DECK of a luxury ship named *Sea Maiden*, occasionally peeking out over the rails and staring at the cerulean water beneath her. She was excited to get home to her mother. It was true that staying with her favorite aunt in the colonies was fun, but after a while she had become impatient to return to the familiar setting of her family's house in England.

It was almost perfect timing when her father arrived in the *Sea Maiden*, along with several other important business men. The *Sea Maiden* had been delayed as a giant storm swept over the American coast. After bidding goodbye to her aunt, Alice boarded and was on her way. For a moment she could forget about home as she became accustomed to the strange life aboard the ship, and spend time with her beloved father, who was constantly called away on business.

Now Alice gazed out at the horizon. She could faintly see something in the distance. The *Sea Maiden* was set on a course to pass just in front of it. As they drew nearer, the ten year old wondered with excitement if the object was another ship. Just as she thought this, the cry came from the watch up the mast.

"Ship from the north!"

All eyes turned upward to the sailor who was now pointing at the distant vessel. Just as quickly, all eyes then turned to the oncoming ship.

Alice found her father and stuck to his side. "What ship is that?"

Her father was silent, so she repeated her question. He finally looked down at Alice and smiled reassuringly. "I'm not sure. But don't worry, darling. It's probably just a merchant ship with fresh cargo."

Alice turned to see what the captain of the *Sea Maiden* was doing. She saw him point to a sailor and then to the mast, but she couldn't hear what he was saying. The sailor hurried to the mast and started raising the Union Jack.

The other ship was a lot closer. Alice could make out people on board, although details were still hazy. It was moving fast, she thought. But neither of the ships had altered their course, so it was obvious they wouldn't collide. The other ship would pass in behind the *Sea Maiden*. Alice thought that was good news, and she found hope in the blue, red, and white flag that now towered above her.

Then the other ship started raising its own flag. Alice watched intently, hoping to see an identical Union Jack. But of the three British colors, only one met her eyes: Red.

There was a collective gasp from the assembled crew and passengers. Her father suddenly grabbed Alice's hand and drew her away from the rail and the other ship.

"What is it, Father?" Alice asked. She could now hear the captain clearly shouting his orders. But not just to the sailors, to the soldiers standing by, as well.

"That ship does not carry friends, Alice, dear," her father said nervously. He knelt down in front of his daughter and turned her so that she was faced away from the red-flagged ship.

"Who are they?"

"They mean to hurt us. But I won't let any harm come to you. I promise, Alice, you will be safe."

Alice could see the determination and the love in her father's eyes. Her father had never lied to her. She trusted him, and she believed every word he spoke.

"But who are they, Father?" Alice insisted. She couldn't see what was going on, but she could hear the soldiers running about, their armor and weapons clanking. It was obvious the red-flagged ship was going to attack, but even she, a mere ten year old, had seen how fortified the *Sea Maiden* was and how difficult it would be to obtain a victory over her.

Her father put a protective arm around Alice and pulled her in close to him. She placed her head on his chest and listened to his great heartbeat quicken as the ship grew closer. He barely whispered into her ear as though the words themselves would doom his daughter.

"They're pirates. Very desperate pirates."

And as he spoke those words, a loud boom shattered the ocean, rocking the *Sea Maiden* violently as the pirates' cannonballs struck her. An earsplitting crack came from the rudder. Alice and her father were thrown to the deck. They clutched each other, one protectively and the other out of fear, as the *Sea Maiden* slowed. Alice peeked over her shoulder to see a dragon figurehead looming above her.

The thunderous shots of firearms could be heard from everywhere on both ships. At one point a couple of cannons fired point blank at the pirate ship. But it was too late to force the pirates away. They were already too close to the *Sea Maiden* by the time they identified themselves, and the momentary panic they caused coupled with the speed at which their ship travelled gave them enough time to get in close before a counterattack could be assembled.

Alice clearly heard the shouts of the captain and commander as they relayed orders to the *Sea Maiden's* crew and soldiers, respectively. She didn't really understand what was being said, but she could tell it was bad news.

"Sir, the rudder has been destroyed! *Sea Maiden* is unable to steer!"

Alice's father scooped her up in his arms and ran to the far side of the ship. Most of the passengers were already there in an attempt to escape from the violence, although there was nowhere to run.

"A red flag!" someone said nervously. "That means no quarter… I thought they stopped using those decades ago!"

Her father set Alice down partly away from the others and put his hands on her shoulders. He looked into her eyes and saw the inevitable tears forming there.

"Listen to me, Alice," he said, his voice rushed but solid. "I want you to hide. Find somewhere on the ship, somewhere no one will find you, and stay there for as long as possible. Do you understand, Alice?" The girl nodded and her father hugged her tight. "You'll be safe. I promise. I love you."

He released her and motioned for her to go. She hesitated and her father gave her an encouraging push. She turned and ran.

A high pitched wailing made Alice turn around. She just had time to see a long chain tumble through the air before it tore at the masts of the *Sea Maiden*, causing splintered wood to fall around her. Some of the sails were now flapping uselessly. The *Sea Maiden* came to a standstill. Alice decided she had better keep moving.

She didn't know where she was going. She had a vague understanding of the ship's layout and figured she was heading toward the back. She could see the red-flagged ship was now parallel to the *Sea Maiden*, its prow alongside the stern at which Alice now stood. She looked out at the dragon figurehead and could read the word "Vengeance" written along the creature's chest.

There were men moving around on the deck of the pirate ship. Some occasionally returned cannon fire as the *Sea Maiden* utilized its heavy artillery, causing the ship to rock as the cannonballs dropped into the nearby water, apparently missing the ship. But Alice could see that ropes slowly drew the *Sea Maiden* to the pirate vessel, and as the two ships came closer the cannon fire ceased. A few pirates were aiming carefully with muskets and firing at specific soldiers as they tried to cut the ropes.

Alice quickly ducked behind some barrels, sure that she would be the next target if she was seen. She covered her face with her hands, wishing only for the horror to end.

The noise and shouting seemed to die down after a few moments. When she looked up again the pirates had boarded the *Sea Maiden* and were using curved swords to hack at any sailors still alive.

Alice watched with renewed fear as the captain of the *Sea Maiden* was confronted. He was unarmed. Two pirates approached him anyway, their swords raised. The captain fell to his knees before them, pleading and begging. The swords came down. Alice looked away and heard the captain's words get cut off.

Alice wiped her eyes on her sleeves. She didn't realize she had started shaking. She had just decided to curl up in a ball when a new sound made her peek out from behind the barrels. Some female survivors were crying with anguish and pain as pirates played with their dresses and hit them. Alice wasn't sure exactly what they were doing, but she could tell that it wasn't good. The rest of the surviving passengers, only a few, her father among them, were being brought to the center of the *Sea Maiden* and assembled around the ruined mast. The passengers were facing her direction, so she had no fear of being spotted by the dreadful pirates.

Two men walked the length of the *Vengeance Dragon*. They crossed the rail and boarded the *Sea Maiden* with an air of authority. One was average height and very muscular with thick arms and broad shoulders. Despite this, it was the other man Alice was drawn to.

He was tall and lean, with ear-length black hair and a clean shaven face of fair complexion. The bones in his face were sharp and prominent, and a bit hollow. And yet there was something about him that invoked both wonder and fear in Alice. There was no hesitation in his stride despite his sunken looks. And he walked with dignity, Alice thought, especially with his tall black boots and lethal rapier at his side that seemed to set him apart from the rest of the pirates. The other man was bigger and stronger, but something told her the consequences of crossing him would be lighter than those of crossing the tall, cold man.

Alice watched as the two men came to a halt in front of the five or so passengers that remained. Alice wondered how so few had survived the pirate attack when the *Sea Maiden* had close to a small army at its disposal. The pirates looked like nothing more than low class vagabonds in their simple clothes. And there were so few of them.

"What should we do with these vermin, Captain?" the strong pirate asked the taller. Alice stared in awe. So this was the captain of the pirate ship and the man responsible for all who had died.

The pirate captain studied his prisoners carefully. He glanced at Alice's father and then briefly scanned the ship he had captured. Alice quickly ducked down before he could spot her. As she straightened back up, she saw that her father was staring at her, his eyes wide. He unobtrusively jerked his head toward the pirate ship. Alice wasn't sure what he meant.

The captain advanced toward Alice's father until they stood just feet apart. He glanced around once more before speaking.

"What's your name?" His voice was just as steady as his walk, but surprisingly low.

The hesitation was only brief. "Thomas Bradford."

Alice was surprised to hear her father sound so calm. He was doing it for her, but she had no idea.

The pirate captain pointed to a wedding ring on Thomas Bradford's finger. "I see that you're married, Mister Bradford." The statement was left hanging. He was obviously waiting for a response.

"Yes, I am married."

"And was your wife on board this vessel when I attacked?"

Thomas Bradford licked his lips. "No, she wasn't."

The captain nodded to himself. "Have you any children, Mister Bradford?"

There was no reply for a while. Thomas Bradford resisted the urge to glance at the spot where he knew his daughter was hiding. He wasn't sure if he should deny having a child but decided that this captain, despite a pirate, was too intuitive to be fooled and not a man to be lied to.

"I have one daughter."

The captain nodded to himself once more. He fingered the hilt of his rapier, apparently unconsciously. "And was she on board?"

Thomas Bradford tried to keep eye contact, to keep his breathing and his voice steady. He didn't dare hope that the captain might be sympathetic for him and his daughter if he told the truth about Alice's whereabouts.

"No."

No one noticed that the captain now had a firm grip on his weapon. "Good for her, then," he muttered carelessly.

The captain gave no warning. He suddenly drew his sword and penetrated Thomas Bradford's chest, letting the thin blade slide between the ribs.

Alice clamped one hand over her mouth to keep from crying out. She watched as the pirate tried to withdraw his sword, only it stuck, so he had to pull on it a second time, finally allowing her father to fall forward upon the deck, one hand clutching his chest. She saw the other, larger pirate smile. Then she saw her father's hand ever so slowly make a fist, minus one finger, so that he was pointing at the pirate ship. The motion was so small that no one noticed, except for Alice.

The captain turned his back on the dead man and nodded to the pirates standing by. There was no emotion on his face. He didn't say anything to them, but they seemed to know what to do, eagerly moving forward to kill the rest of the passengers. Then he walked toward his own ship, ready to board it, when the strong man spoke for the first time.

"Are you sure about that, Stephen?" His voice was loud and even deeper than the captain's. "Ransoming them would pay us good money."

"You're bringing this up now?" The captain's reply was filled with annoyance. "We've been over this before and I don't want to hear it again, especially not from my first mate. The *Vengeance Dragon* sails under the red flag for a reason."

He abruptly made his way back to his own ship, leaving his first mate. Alice looked once more at her dead father and his pointing hand. She finally steeled herself and crawled forward to the pirate ship. She wasn't sure why her father wanted her to board it, but she believed in his promise that she would be safe.

CHAPTER THREE

THE *VENGEANCE DRAGON* HAD a very different layout than the *Sea Maiden*, and so Alice was unsure of where to go. She finally settled down in the prow where some crates formed a small, secluded alcove. It was the best she could hope for. Maybe she wouldn't be discovered at all and when the pirates docked she could make an escape.

Hunkered down and out of sight, Alice didn't bother watching what was going on around her. She could hear the first mate and the few pirates return. She could also hear the sound of rushing water as it filled the *Sea Maiden* and dragged the ship under the water. And she could feel the movement of the *Vengeance Dragon* as it pulled away from the wreckage. But then she heard more sounds, walking and talking, and Alice realized that there were a lot more than a few ragtag pirates on board. However, she didn't dare take a peek for fear of being spotted.

In fact, Alice had never experienced such profound fear. She had seen what that awful pirate captain had done to her father and to the rest of the crew. Every time the sight reentered her mind fresh tears would spill from her already red rimmed eyes. She'd never see her father again. And if she was discovered she'd never see her mother again. Just when she was finally about to return home, home had been snatched away from her. It seemed to her that cargo wasn't the only thing these pirates had stolen.

As the night settled in, Alice shivered uncontrollably. She wrapped her arms around herself in an attempt to keep warm. She spent the night in this way, blanketed in cold fear.

She knew that she would be found eventually. And even if she wasn't found, she would never make her presence known to the pirates. Alice resolved this to herself. She would die of hunger long before she would let them get their hands on her.

However, the moment came early the very next morning. Alice opened her eyes and sat up from the awkward crouch she had been sleeping in, only to find herself face to face with a young man who was on his knees and peeking between the crates.

They both jumped backward from each other and the young man cried out in surprise. Then he immediately covered his mouth with his right hand, his eyes wide.

Alice tried to make herself invisible, wriggling farther into her nook as the young man announced his finding. Before long, a small crowd had gathered around the area, each head craning to catch a glimpse of the stowaway.

The young man had described Alice as a "girl" to his fellow pirates. Now that they could see how young she was, they became outwardly excited. Some reached their hands between the barrels to try to touch her, but she pressed back as far as she could. Others whistled at her as if she might come to them when called like a dog.

Then she heard a deeper voice say, "Out of the way, let me through." The crowd parted to let a man through. It was the same man that had been there when Alice's father was killed, the stronger-built one. The first mate.

He took a good, long look at Alice. She didn't return the eye contact.

"Let me take care of this," he said, and he started moving the crates. His muscles tensed as he slowly heaved them aside one at a time.

Alice started to panic. Aside from wedged among these crates, there was nowhere else for her to run to. She started to cry.

"Shut up!" the first mate shouted with annoyance. He drew his sword, but that only caused Alice to cry louder.

But then a different, silent man approached the crates. He parted the crowd without saying a word. If Alice had been fearful before, she was horrified now. A frozen terror grasped her in icy fingers. She stopped crying but the tears were still on her face and the panic was still in her chest. The man now standing before her was the man that had killed her father, and his hand was resting on the killing weapon itself, buckled to his side.

The pirate captain stood in front of the crates, towering over Alice and studying her with empty eyes. His blue eyes looked black, like the kind of ice that only makes itself known once someone has already stepped on it and fallen as a result.

No one moved, least of all Alice. She felt that the longer the captain looked at her, the colder she became, and he seemed to look at her forever, like his icy stare was freezing time itself.

After an eternity, after Alice had finally begun to find the silence unbearable, the pirate spoke.

"Come here."

He did not say it very loudly and it did not hold any kind of energy. In fact, his voice was rather unremarkable, the complete opposite of what Alice had expected after being tortured by his eyes. Yet after all that silence the two words spoken with indifference cut through her as if they had been shouted at her with vehement impatience.

Alice did not move. The first mate released a chuckle. The captain spared him a glance, silencing him immediately.

The captain squatted down. His sword was so long that it scraped the deck as he did so. Now at eye level, Alice was even more unnerved, so she avoided looking at his face.

"Come here," he said again, this time with some emphasis. He reached his hand between the crates. A couple of feet separated them, even with his hand outstretched, but Alice squirmed backward all the same.

"Listen to me," the captain said, letting just a bit of urgency to creep into his voice. "If you come with me now, I can guarantee that no harm will come to you. Otherwise, I will tell my first mate to resume moving the crates and he will do so gladly. If he gets to you first I don't know what he'll do, but I'm certain your safety is not one of his top concerns."

The first mate chuckled again.

Still not looking at the captain, Alice asked in a voice so wavering that she had to repeat the question in order to be heard clearly, "Do you care about my safety?"

"No," he replied. "I'm just curious to know how you got here. I'd rather have such a conversation in my cabin where we'll be free from these nosy men." As he said this he turned to look at the men behind him for their amusement and they all grinned.

Alice did not want to talk to this man, let alone have a private conversation with him. But just as she had gambled to board the pirate vessel in the first place, she decided that her chances were better with him than with the first mate. Slowly, she nodded to the captain. He stood up and stepped back to allow Alice to crawl forward.

Before she knew it, he had clamped his hand around her wrist in an iron grip and yanked her to her feet none too gently.

The captain started to drag her away when the first mate stopped him. "What are you going to do?"

"I'm going to have a chat."

The captain didn't wait for a reply. He walked past his first mate, Alice in tow. She had trouble keeping up with his long strides, but his hand on her wrist kept her from falling behind.

He led her to the stern of the ship where the entrance to the captain's cabin was. He roughly pulled her inside and then finally let go of her, the momentum of the movement causing her to stumble, but she did not fall. She stood awkwardly in the middle of the room as the captain closed the door.

The room was rather bare. There were several shelves lining the walls, each full of stacks of bound paper. Opposite the main door was another entryway to a smaller room, but Alice couldn't see inside. A couple of storage trunks sat around the room. There was also a low, wide desk in one corner, and a liquor cabinet in another. Several small windows lined the outside walls. The captain had taken a seat on the desk's edge. From there he eyed her and she felt uncomfortably exposed under his gaze.

"What's your name?" he said at last, and although he said it as a question, Alice could hear no curiosity in his voice. She didn't answer, so he asked instead, "Did you come from the last ship we attacked? What was it called... the *Sea Maiden*?"

Alice nodded.

"And what possibly gave you the idea to come aboard my ship?"

This time when she didn't answer, the captain did not ask a different question. He just continued to look at her, clearly waiting for her to speak. He never repeated the question, so Alice said very quietly, "My father."

"Smart man. You've most certainly outlived everyone else that was on that ship. What was his name?"

At that moment Alice very strongly did not want to talk to the captain anymore. The way he said *was* rather than *is* without even thinking about it, it made her feel ill. She thought that she was about to be killed. Once the thought entered her head, the room around her became fuzzy and started to spin. Alice swayed on her feet.

The captain took a step toward her and put his hand on her shoulder. Although his grip kept her on her feet, it hurt her. She cringed at his touch and tried to remain still. But then his other hand dropped to his sword, causing Alice to push away from him in a terror, falling over in the process.

"His name is Thomas Bradford!" she cried desperately. "Please, don't!"

The captain looked down at his hand and seemed to notice for the first time that he was gripping his sword. He released it and backed away from Alice, realizing that she thought he would kill her for not answering his questions.

"I'm not going to harm you," he said.

She didn't believe him and he could tell. After a moment's hesitation, he unbuckled the sword from his side and set it on the desk.

"I remember your father," he told her, trying to sound gentle and failing.

"Of course you remember him. You killed him!" Alice blurted. "I saw you do it, and now you're going to kill me too!" She tried to hold back the tears but couldn't. She saw the terrible moment happen all over again.

The door to the cabin opened and the first mate entered without knocking. "What's going on? I heard shouting." He looked around the room and noticed that Alice was on the floor against one wall while the captain stood near the opposite wall. He smirked at the captain. "Having a chat, are you? I know ransoming is out of the question, so let me be done with her and get this over with."

"I don't want to kill her, Richard," the captain said sternly.

"Never thought I'd ever hear you say that. What is it you even want from her, anyway?"

"I'm just trying to get answers."

The first mate gave a deep, belly laugh. "And how's that going for you?" He leaned over Alice menacingly. "You know what we do to people who don't answer our questions, girl?"

Alice scrambled away from him while the first mate laughed. The captain, not giving the torment any heed, said, "But think about it, Richard. A young girl who just lost her father, comes aboard the responsible ship? Not many people would do that." He spoke as if Alice wasn't present.

The first mate seemed to follow the captain's line of thinking. He asked Alice, "How old are you, girl? Twelve?"

She quietly answered, "Ten." Both men reacted with mild amazement.

The first mate swung his gaze over to the captain. "So are you going to cut her loose or should I?"

The captain shook his head thoughtfully. "She'll stay with me a little longer."

"Alright," the first mate said, becoming serious. "I hope you know what you're doing." He let himself out.

Alice and the captain remained on their respective sides of the cabin for what seemed like a long time in silence. Alice had stopped crying and she now sat with her knees drawn up to her chest while the captain leaned against his desk.

Finally, the captain said, "You're the first person to have stowed away on this ship since I became its captain eight years ago." He waited for a response. When there wasn't one, he continued talking in a conversational tone. "You gave Wistar quite a start, I've been told. He's the one that found you. He's no pirate. Just a fiddler." Still she said nothing. "Will you not speak to me?"

At that, Alice looked up at him. She thought for sure that she would see anger or impatience, but she saw only a genuine interest in the things he had said.

"I want to go home," she sobbed. "Please, I'll do anything. Just let me go."

"I can't let you go. It wouldn't be safe for me."

"I don't understand."

The captain thought carefully for a moment. He seemed to be trying to formulate a simplified explanation in his head. When that failed, he said instead, "My name's Stephen Boswell. What's yours?"

"Alice Bradford." Her voice shook.

"Well, Miss Bradford, I'm giving you a chance to live, so long as you do as you're told." He buckled his sword back on as he spoke. He nodded toward the back room. "There's a bed in there you can use. Now I need to go speak to my men."

The captain strode out of the cabin without a backward glance. His crew was working dutifully, yet they cast curious glances at him when they saw him. He knew what they wondered about. He walked with purpose up to the quarter deck where they would be able to see him better and called out, "I need your attention." The men paused in whatever they had been doing and turned to face their captain.

Captain Boswell cleared his throat. "I'll make this quick. The stowaway's name is Alice Bradford. She came from the *Sea Maiden*. I'm letting her live for now. I don't expect her presence to cause any problems as she'll be staying with me." He paused. "That is all."

The men returned to their duties efficiently, chatting amongst themselves about this unprecedented turn of events. Captain Boswell returned to the cabin and glanced toward the small bedroom at the back. Alice sat on the edge of his bed and stared at the floor. He didn't pay much attention to her and sat at his desk. The list of inventory from the *Sea Maiden* sat before him and he looked over it, figuring out what to trade and what to keep and how to split it evenly among his crew. He hadn't gotten far when someone knocked on the door.

"Come in," he called without looking up. The ship's cook, Philip Reuben, entered. He held a plate of food in his hand.

"I brought something for the little lady to eat." His voice was thick and rough and held a hint of a northern accent.

Captain Boswell jerked his head toward the bedroom. "She's in there."

As Reuben approached her, Alice couldn't help but sweep her eyes from his feet to the top of his head. He lurched with every step that he took, the limp stemming from his right leg. He was a rather large man and seemed to take up a lot of space in the room. His hair and beard were long and almost completely gray. His face was weathered and lined with deep creases and crow's feet touched the corners of his eyes. He was smiling widely.

"Hello, the name's Reuben. Brought you some food." He set down the plate next her. It contained only some greens and what appeared to be stale bread. Alice tried not to show her dissatisfaction. "If you need anything else, just ask." Then he lowered his voice. "Don't let the captain scare you, little lady."

Captain Boswell's voice carried over. "Are you talking about me, Reuben?" He almost sounded amused.

"Oh, not at all." Reuben winked at Alice and she allowed herself to smile a little, which caused Reuben's smile to widen even more which hadn't seemed possible beforehand. Reuben hobbled out of the room.

"Need anything, Captain?" Reuben asked as he continued on to the door of the cabin.

"No, thank you, Reuben."

"I'll be off, then. Back to the prow. The long, difficult walk to the prow."

Captain Boswell grinned and shook his head. Reuben let out a guffaw before leaving.

Alice looked down at the food that Reuben had brought. Her stomach rumbled despite the food's repulsive appearance. She ate all of it very quickly. Then she glanced at the captain. He was occupied by his papers. Alice didn't know what to do with herself. She lifted her legs onto the bed, tucked them beneath her, and simply sat, wondering how long she would be prisoner here.

CHAPTER FOUR

A FEW DAYS PASSED. Alice spent the nights in the captain's room at the back of the cabin, sleeping in his bed while he took to the chair at his desk. She never came out of the room and he never really told her that she could, but she didn't want to test if there would be consequences for doing so. She was always alone, and she always kept the door closed. The only time she saw the captain was when he brought her food and when he retrieved some of his things from the room, as need for them arose.

The food he brought was simple and tasteless. It was nothing like what she had on the *Sea Maiden*. And there was not much fresh water onboard. Anything given to her to drink had some sort of alcohol mixed in with it, making it disgusting to drink.

Alice passed the time by reading the captain's books and looking through his belongings. He had a lot. Some books contained logs from the ships he had attacked, as well as records of inventory that the pirates had stolen. Others contained stories. Those were Alice's favorite, although she also enjoyed looking at the ones filled with maps. The *Vengeance Dragon*'s log was among the papers she found, or at least parts of it, written in the captain's own hand. Of the captain's belongings, most of it was clothes. The rest were trinkets, but the room was small, and so there was not much else. There was more in the main room, she knew, by his desk.

Occasionally Alice would hear voices on the other side of the door and listen in. She heard the first mate a lot. She learned his name was Richard Titus. His voice was loud and he was always complaining about something, either the weather or problems with the men or anything, really. Alice could never hear the captain well because he spoke so softly.

She slept restlessly. Nightmares kept her awake. During the second night she risked to leave the room, just needing a change of scenery. But upon creeping open the door and peeping through the crack, she saw the captain sleeping in his chair and changed her mind.

After the third night, when Alice woke in the morning, she knew she couldn't stay cooped up any longer. She was both restless and exhausted. She heard the captain's footsteps approach the door, knowing that he was bringing breakfast. *Be bold*, she thought, and opened the door before he could.

Captain Boswell had a cup and eating utensils in his left hand and a plate balanced on his arm. His right hand was extended toward the door knob. He wore a stunned expression on his face.

"I want to eat out here," Alice rushed to say. And then she added with authority, "Please."

She saw the captain lift his eyebrows in exasperation. He didn't say anything, but he turned around and placed the meal on his desk across from his own and sat. Alice tentatively approached the desk, but there was only one chair and so she awkwardly stood by, glancing between the food and the captain, who had already begun to eat.

"Bring that trunk over to sit on," he told her at last, nodding toward an ornate, wooden chest in the corner. Alice stuck her hand through a loop on the side of the chest and gave it a tug to feel its weight. It didn't budge, so she grasped it with both hands and leaned back, trying to pull it with her full strength. Captain Boswell sighed audibly. He got up, shooed her away, and dragged the chest over with one hand. Then he promptly sat down again and resumed eating.

Alice seated herself, as well. She stole a glance at the captain before picking up a fork and digging in. Several minutes went by in silence. Neither one of them looked at the other. Alice took a sip from her cup, making a sour face at the boozy taste. Captain Boswell allowed just his eyes to lift to catch the expression. It seemed he might give a remark, but he was interrupted by a knock at the door.

The captain hardly twitched. "Enter." He was a little surprised to see Titus. His first mate never knocked before entering and was the only crewmember to get away with it.

"A ship's been spotted, sailing from the west," Titus explained. "She's a trader, definitely returning to Europe with a full cargo, exactly what we need."

"Don't raise the flag," Captain Boswell ordered. "We'll take her by surprise. Ready the men. I'll be there shortly."

Titus gave a nod and left. Standing, the captain turned to Alice.

"Stay here," he told her meaningfully as he put on his sword, gun, and coat. "Do not leave the cabin. Keep the door closed." He gave her a stern look before following after his first mate. Alice had no intentions of obeying him. She eased the door open, glanced left then right, and slipped out onto the deck.

She saw Captain Boswell standing at the bulwarks midship with Titus and two other men. The rest of the crew ran about, some readying weapons as others prepared ropes and adjusted the sails. Alice took a moment to observe the pirates, this being her first chance to do so. Most wore basic shoes and plain clothing, simple sailor's outfits. Their ages constituted a wide range from twenty to forty, although most were closer to the young end of the spectrum. If she hadn't known that this was a pirate vessel, Alice would have mistaken those men for simple merchants, and relatively poor ones at that.

Alice saw the trading ship in the distance slowly grow closer to the *Vengeance Dragon*. She remembered the day that her position had been in the reverse, with the *Vengeance Dragon* bearing down on her and her father.

The trading vessel raised its flag and Alice saw the red and yellow of the Spanish flag. She watched Captain Boswell, who seemed to be judging distances very carefully. After some time, he made a hand signal and the dreaded red pirate flag rose up the mast. He then turned to one of the men next to him and spoke a few words. The man nodded and ran off below deck.

Alice could imagine the panic that was spreading on the innocent trading ship. She could see its captain desperately shouting orders and pointing out to the open sea. The ship started to turn away from the pirates, apparently following his orders, when a loud boom went off. A second later there sounded splintering wood from the trader. It stopped turning. Alice knew right away that her rudder had been destroyed, the memory of it on the *Sea Maiden* all too vivid in her mind.

Return fire rocked the *Vengeance Dragon* and Alice pressed her hands against the wall behind her to stay steady. Ropes flew from the *Vengeance Dragon* and secured the trader. Gunshots could be heard all along the decks of both ships. A number of pirates drew curved swords and jumped onto the deck of the trader. The scene was horrid in Alice's eyes. The rogues hacked away at sailors like ferocious animals, hardly hesitating between victims. The screams of the sailors, both those that fought back and those that fled, overwhelmed the young girl. She looked instead at Captain Boswell, but his calm and almost bored composure sickened her just as much as the massacre.

When the fray had calmed down, Alice snuck to the middle of the main deck of the *Vengeance Dragon* to better hear what was going on. Captain Boswell and Titus had just crossed over to the trader when she found a decent hiding place. The position she now found herself in seemed ironic to her after everything she had been through.

There were only three survivors and they were on their knees. The dead bodies were dragged to the prow of the trader, their persons searched for any valuables. These sailors, despite their guns, had been attacked when they were virtually defenseless and largely outnumbered.

Captain Boswell and Titus approached the three men. The captain nodded to his first mate, and Titus raised his sword.

"Who speaks English?" he hollered. The three cringed, but only one looked down. Titus grabbed him by the shirt, pulled him to his feet, and laid his sword on the poor man's shoulder. "You speak English, huh?"

The sailor nodded vigorously as if he hoped his knowledge of the language would save his life. Titus pushed him back into his comrades. He pointed to one of the others.

"Is he the captain?"

It was obvious that the man was, in fact, the captain from his dress. The sailor acknowledged anyway and nodded again. Captain Boswell glanced over his shoulder at two of his crewmembers. Apparently no words were needed, for they grabbed the Spanish captain by the arms and hair and slit his throat without warning. Captain Boswell then walked up to the English speaking sailor until only a couple of feet separated them. He drew his rapier very deliberately and pressed the point under his chin. The poor man was horror-stricken and trembling all over.

"This is a Spanish blade," Captain Boswell mused. Alice couldn't believe how resigned his voice sounded. "I took it from a ship just like yours years ago." And he pressed the tip through the man's throat, prompting a whoop from the nearby pirates who immediately attacked the last man while he begged in his native tongue for mercy. Captain Boswell remained impassive, even as the English speaker writhed and choked to death on his own blood.

Alice felt herself shaking all over. She felt that she had now seen Captain Boswell for who he truly was: not a man, but an animal. A predator.

She saw the captain and first mate return to the *Vengeance Dragon*. Captain Boswell was saying something about trading in everything they had confiscated from the Spanish trader and the *Sea Maiden*. There was no guilt in his voice, or remorse or horror. He was completely unfazed and unemotional.

Alice stood up abruptly. She didn't care if anyone saw her. Captain Boswell would probably kill her anyway. Scanning the world about her, all she saw was water. There was nothing. She stood on the vessel, trapped, and panic bubbled up from inside her. She ran across the main deck to the cabin, flew open the door, slammed it closed behind her, and flung herself onto the captain's bed in the next room. She buried her face in her arms.

Captain Boswell saw her run across the deck. He swore under his breath, and Titus smirked.

"You're right, she is an interesting girl, Stephen," the first mate joked.

Captain Boswell ignored him. "Just do your job, Richard. I'll deal with her." He left his first mate standing there, the smirk still evident on his face.

Alice heard the captain enter the cabin, his heavy boots making resounding thuds on the planking. She sat up, her eyes widening with fright. His footsteps paused and the sound of rasping metal followed. He had evidently drawn his sword. On the bed, Alice scooted back against the wall and pulled her knees to her chest. She considered pulling the sheets over her head, but decided that she would rather see the captain coming.

She expected to see his sword point round the corner first, but even so its presence stunned and frightened her. He stepped into the bedroom and stopped. Alice tried to be brave and glared at him, although her eyes had filled with tears during his approach.

"I didn't want you to see any of that," Captain Boswell said quietly. He searched Alice's face for some kind of reply, but there was none. "That's why I told you to stay here."

"What do you care?" Her voice wavered, yet her declaration was still sharp.

"Children shouldn't have to witness the deaths of others."

"Well, you should've thought of that when you killed my father!"

The captain was startled at her ferocity. For a moment he was silent. He squinted his eyes at her, inspecting her. It made her uncomfortable.

"I didn't know you were present when I killed your father," he said.

Alice hated how impassive he seemed. "So if you had known I was there, you wouldn't have killed him?"

She continued to glare accusatory at him. They both knew the outcome would have been the same. However, Captain Boswell knew it more than her. As she watched, his eyes drifted away from her and he seemed to lose focus on the present. For just a moment he became lost in his own mind. He saw his own hand holding a pistol, smoke escaping from its barrel. And a man on a nearby ship, falling, a bloody hole in his head.

The captain shook his head briefly, snapping out of it. The knuckles on the hand that held his sword had turned white. He loosened his grip. He seemed bothered and abruptly took a step toward Alice.

Alice couldn't help it. She yelled at him, "What you did to those people is horrible!"

He froze immediately and snapped at her, "I did it for my men."

"It doesn't matter. It's evil." Her words had an effect. The captain stiffened, the muscles in his face tightening. Somehow this gave Alice confidence. Seeing emotion in him, even anger, revealed to her that he was not completely inhuman. The fire he displayed now was not as threatening as his cool. Alice managed to hold eye contact with him, even as he barked at her.

"Don't pretend to understand anything I do!"

After a few seconds of glaring at her and apparently trying to think of something else to say, he stormed out of the room and slammed the door behind him. However, he used such force that instead of closing properly, the door bounced back open. The captain ignored it and left the cabin. Alice smirked, feeling that she had won a small victory.

CHAPTER FIVE

~ 1709 ~

WHEN MY FATHER RETURNED HOME as he did every few months, he was too late. The illness had taken my mother's life. We couldn't afford the medicine that may have been able to save her. We also had no way of contacting my father who may have been able to pay for it. But that's what a life of piracy does, doesn't it? It tears families apart.

He returned to a house occupied by only me. He asked where Mother was. I told him the graveyard.

He offered to give me enough money to give myself a life, to continue living in the house without worrying about losing it. I told him I didn't want it.

"I'm sorry I wasn't here to help buy the medicine, Stephen," he said.

I replied coolly, "Mother deserved better than blood money anyway."

I packed a bag of some clothes and food, only enough to last a couple of days, really. Father stood by and watched. We didn't have much in the house. I was hardly leaving anything behind.

"Sell the house if you want to," I said as I walked by him to the door. "I won't be needing it and you hardly use it anyway. Now's your chance to make some honest money."

I reached for the doorknob, but before I could turn it and pull open the door, Father clasped my forearm.

"Stephen, please," he begged. "Where will you go? What will you do?"

Truthfully, I was unsure. Maybe I was acting rashly. But maybe not. "I'll go anywhere and do anything. I'll find work. I'll earn my keep."

"Stephen." I heard my father's tone change. He seemed less self-assured as he voiced his next thought. "Why don't you come with me?"

I turned sharply, causing him to let go of my arm, and faced him directly for the first time since he had returned. "Go with you?" I tried to muster a mocking laugh, but couldn't. I was just too hurt. "I will never go with you. I will never become a pirate."

I angrily stared him in the eye for about a second. The anger burned inside me. It was painful. I didn't let him reply. I stormed out, slamming the door shut behind me. I left the house at a brisk walk, wiping my eyes since they had started to sting.

I was determined to live an honest life, to refrain from growing up to be like my father, from going on the account. That determination was what led me out into the world, completely alone, for the first time. I was sixteen years old at the time. And I had no idea how wrong I would be.

CHAPTER SIX

~ 1710 ~

MOSTLY I TRAVELLED ALONG THE WATERFRONT. I didn't regret leaving, nor the words I had said to my father. Yet I suppose some part of me wanted that familiarity of being near water, reminding me of home.

I performed odd jobs for the seafaring people of England. I did everything from cleaning the undersides of boats to helping women with their household chores while their husbands went out fishing. In return I would be given two meals, one before bed and one the next morning. Some folks made me work again the next day before letting me have breakfast. Those deals were unfair, sure, but I took everything I could get, never knowing when I'd be able to get another one again.

Usually I slept in a shed or barn out back if the family had one. Sometimes in the cellar. Twice I did work for some rich people and was awarded with entry to the servants' quarters. And once I was given the spare bedroom. I stayed at that house for two nights instead of my typical one. I was even asked to stay a third night, but I denied the offer. I was on a strict regimen with myself.

I didn't want to stay in one place too long because I was afraid someone would find out that my father was a pirate. I knew logically that it was impossible, that only I would be able to give myself away. And I knew that there would be no real consequences if they did find out. Maybe a little hate or distrust, maybe a backing out on a deal they had made with me, but nothing travelling to the next town couldn't fix.

I guess I was just trying to run away from the truth. If I could travel fast enough, spending as little time as possible in one place while still earning a living, then the memory of everything I had left behind in that house wouldn't be able to catch up with me.

A year of living like this passed when it finally did.

"Stephen?"

I had finished some morning work down at the docks and was walking back along the pier when I heard my name. A sloop had pulled in. Turning to face it and looking for the source of the voice, I saw my father.

"Stephen!" he said again, this time with excited recognition.

I shook my head and hurried along the pier. I heard the thud of boots hitting wood and knew that he had jumped from his vessel to pursue me. His hand touched my shoulder.

"Stephen, wait."

I shrugged his hand off.

"Please."

I stopped, took a quick deep breath, and then turned to face him. He was smiling with thrilled astonishment, his hands out like he couldn't believe it was me, but thrilled that it was at the same time. I couldn't bear for him to look at me like that.

"You look older," he finally said.

His words prompted me to look at him more closely. He also looked older. His beard was fuller than I last remembered it, and almost entirely gray. His skin had yellowed and seemed to cling to him.

All I wanted was to walk away, to leave him behind, to never see him again. He stood there in front of me, happy to see me, everything he had done still fresh in my mind as if it had happened yesterday, and I just couldn't do it.

"Just leave me alone," I spat.

"Stephen…." The hurt was evident.

"Stop saying my name." I took a step back and stared at the ground.

"Alright," he said, reserved. "You know, I… I am sorry for not coming home sooner. Last time when… when your mother was ill."

"I know when!" I snapped, not wanting to remember. "If you think saying sorry can fix it, you're wrong. If you think being late that time was your only mistake, you're terribly wrong."

"How could I have known that she was sick? You blame me but there's no way I could have been there sooner if I didn't know."

"You could have known if you hadn't left in the first place," I growled.

Father quietly reasoned, "Then tell me how to fix everything."

I laughed. Finally, after a year, it came out. "That's just it, Father. You can't fix it. The damage has been done. There is absolutely nothing you can do but get back on that sloop and let it take you to the hidden pirate ship I know is waiting for you. Go kill some innocent people, go steal all their belongings, go destroy someone else's life!"

Father crossed his arms. "So that's what this is about?"

"This is what it has always been about!" I shouted. "You weren't just late to save Mother, you were late every day that you weren't home with us! And the days that you were home, I hardly knew who you were. You always claimed that you were living a better life, that you had become a free man. I don't believe living a life separate from family can be better, and I don't believe that killing and robbing people can equate to freedom."

It was then that my father's eyes narrowed. He took a step closer to me, his face leaning over mine threateningly. "Don't presume to understand what you don't, boy," he growled. "You know nothing of this world. You blindly do as you're told, stand aside when someone better than you walks by, accept the authority of others simply because of the fancy clothes they wear." His voice quickened and reached a terrifying crescendo. "You have no idea what men are really like. You're just a beggar. You're just a rat living in the gutter, letting others step on you with their shiny shoes!"

"Shut your mouth!" I cried. "Shut it!" And then, before I could stop myself, before I could let Father's words get to me, I let out the words that I kept silent all this time as pathetic tears sprung to my eyes. "It's your fault… all of it! I blame you for everything! My mother is dead because of-"

Father's hand flew through the air faster than I could fathom. The knuckles of his backhanded slap collided with my cheek. I recoiled from the strike, replacing what would have been the last word of my sentence with an involuntary gasp. I slowly raised my eyes to look at him without moving my head. He pointed a finger sternly at me.

"Don't you dare finish that sentence," he spat. "You are weak. One day you'll understand everything. You'll see the world for what it really is. You'll be stepped on like you never have been before. You'll get crushed. And then you'll want to fight back. You'll see."

For the first time, my father walked away from me. He left me standing on the dock as he made his way back to his sloop. And as he walked, he casually said over his shoulder, "When it happens, be sure to remember this."

I turned and ran.

CHAPTER SEVEN

ALICE HAD BEEN DRIFTING off to sleep when she felt the pirate ship come to a halt. She sat up in surprise and rubbed the sleep out of her eyes. The ship had never stopped while she was on board, only to attack the Spanish trader. She poked her head out of the bedroom. The captain was at his desk, as usual. A small lamp illuminated the cabin.

"What's happened?" she dared to ask him.

He didn't look up from his papers. "We've stopped to trade in our merchandise for more reasonable cargo."

Alice flinched at the word merchandise. Is that how these pirates thought of their stolen goods?

"You'll be arrested as soon as you set foot on land," Alice told him smugly. She immediately regretted the words. But the captain didn't seem to notice her tone of voice. She was starting to wonder if she could use this stop to her advantage.

"We've arrived at a pirate's haven," he explained, unfolding a map and smoothing it onto his desk. Alice eagerly walked over to look at it with him, and then silently scolded herself for acting too enthusiastic. She didn't want the captain to catch on to what she was thinking.

Captain Boswell pointed to a small island. "We're here, at the dock of this northern Caribbean island. It would take one large army to arrest us."

"Are you going to shore?" she asked a little too quickly. But even as he answered she knew he was too preoccupied by his papers to notice.

"No, Reuben takes care of all transactions for me."

Alice was disappointed at that. There was no possible way to sneak out while the captain was sitting right there.

The captain had barely looked up once from the paperwork scattered across his desk. Alice continued to stand there, clasping and unclasping her hands, wondering what to do. Several minutes passed in uncomfortable silence. Captain Boswell kept his eyes down, yet his hands fidgeted. Eventually he breathed deeply and it seemed that he might speak when the door opened.

His head snapped up and Alice took a step back. Titus entered the cabin with an agitated face.

"It's Reed. He wants to meet with you." Titus was obviously annoyed and both the captain and Alice could hear it in his voice.

Captain Boswell scowled. "Did he give a reason?"

"He won't agree to any offer Reuben gives him. He thinks there's some sort of cheat going on or something.

That ass. Either he's found us out and wants the bounty or he truly is backing out of our arrangement."

"Either way, we're going to have to find a new dealer," Captain Boswell said, standing up. "Reuben is still with him?"

"Yeah, still trying to make a deal, just to keep him from getting suspicious."

The captain gathered his sword and pistol as Titus said, "I'll meet you on the pier, Stephen." On his way out, Alice could hear him mutter "that ass" once more under his breath. As soon as he had gone, she turned to the captain.

"What's going on?" Alice was hopeful.

"We just need to go take care of someone." He put on his frockcoat and headed to the door.

"You mean kill."

Captain Boswell paused to look at her and said condescendingly, "Yes. Now stay in this cabin."

Once he had gone, Alice steadied herself and made her decision. She slipped on her shoes then allowed several seconds to pass before moving to the door.

She peeked out of the cabin and could see the captain depart from the ship with his first mate. She also saw the captain look back briefly at the cabin door which she quickly shut. A few seconds later she allowed herself to open it a crack once again. Both of the men were gone. Her chance had finally come.

Alice opened the door a little wider, just enough for her to poke her head outside. There were not many pirates out and none seemed to be paying attention to her, so she slipped out and closed the door behind her. Then she stole along the side of the ship and went down the gangplank onto solid ground.

She did it. She escaped. Alice took a deep breath, feeling the relief overwhelm her. Now all she had to do was figure out where she was and then get home. It couldn't be that hard. There were a number of other ships lining the dock. Surely one of their captains would agree to take her. Of course, she'd have to wait until the morning to ask. Showing up at this hour with such a request might hinder an agreement.

Alice ventured into the town. There was a very light drizzle of rain stirring up a fog that caused Alice to shiver. Her dress was quickly dampening. The farther she walked from the ship, the more she realized how alone she was and how dark and eerie the town seemed. She quickened her pace, hoping to find an inn or something of the likes to take shelter in.

Alice had walked down a couple of streets when she heard a voice that, despite its low tone, made her jump. "Hey, little girl!"

She turned around to see a young man coming towards her. His long blond hair and slight stubble lined a hardened, handsome face. But what she noticed most about him was the sly smile that scarred his face. She was at first relieved to see him, but when she saw that smile she became suddenly afraid.

"Hey, little girl," he said again, this time with a hint of mockery. "What're you doing out here all by yourself, hm?" He was walking faster now.

Alice promptly turned and started walking back the way she had come. She tried not to be urgent but stay calm. However, her attempt failed when she realized that he was right behind her.

He put a hand on her shoulder and she let out a little yelp. When she tried to get away, he grasped her tightly. When she tried to pry his hand with her own, he dug his fingers into her flesh and pushed her roughly against a wall.

"Stop!" Alice cried out desperately. Her outcry only caused him to squeeze tighter.

"Now, now, just hold still," he cooed. The stench coming from his mouth was almost unbearable. He started sliding his forefinger down the side of Alice's face as his tongue simultaneously slid across his bottom lip.

Alice's voice shook as she spoke. "Please, just let me go."

"Well, you can plead all you want, little girl," he snarled. His finger went down her neck to the neckline of her dress. Now Alice tried not to panic. She didn't fully understand exactly what he intended, but she had seen it happen to the female victims of the *Sea Maiden* and knew that it was evil.

Alice tried to push past him but he was too strong, pushing her harder and harder against the wall. Then she kicked him in the shin. He certainly felt it, but it didn't seem to faze him.

Desperately, she kicked him again. It was a mistake. He pulled a knife and pressed it against her throat.

"Now," he said slowly, "you're going to stop struggling or you're going to feel a little prickle. "I'm gonna put this away now, and you're not going to kick me again, you understand?"

Before waiting for an answer, he moved the knife down to her collarbone and let its point sink slowly into her flesh, drawing blood. Alice bit down on her tongue to keep from crying out. She had never felt this kind of pain before.

"So, you understand, don't you?" the man said, repeating his question.

Alice nodded as tears fell from her eyes. She didn't make a sound, but she was shaking slightly. The man put the knife back into his jacket and put his hand at the bottom of her neck again. She could have tried to get away again. She could have kicked and pulled and fought, but she was just too scared. There was a dull pain in her back from constantly hitting the wall. She just couldn't bring herself to do anything. The man started tearing the front of her dress very carefully and suddenly she was seeing her father get stabbed through the chest by the quick thrust of a pirate captain's sword. The fear that oppressed her at that moment was unlike any fear she had ever felt before. So she accepted the man's threat and stopped resisting.

And suddenly Alice heard the muffled sound of two bodies colliding as the man was body slammed by another, the force sending both of them to the ground. Alice also toppled over, but she quickly scurried away from the two men that were now grappling violently with each other and was about to stand and run when she saw Richard Titus standing a few feet away.

He was watching the skirmish, and when Alice saw him she froze. She slowly turned to look back at the fighting men and realized that the one that had just freed her was Captain Boswell. Right now he was struggling against the other man, each trying to gain the upper hand, and it appeared he was losing.

Alice looked desperately from the Captain to his first mate, surprised at her wish for Titus to do something to help Captain Boswell. But he only stood there and watched. Alice also stood there and watched; it was all she could do, even as the man struck the captain's face with a solid fist and pinned him down. She cringed as more blows rained down. Alice could see the toned muscles that defined the man's arms. She had felt their strength firsthand. She knew Captain Boswell was in a bad position.

As Alice continued to watch, she saw the man pull his knife, the same knife that he used to threaten her just moments ago. Without any hesitation at all, without her even fully realizing what was happening, he thrust it downward in a dagger hold.

CHAPTER EIGHT

~ 1711 ~

I WAS BEING WATCHED. I knew it right away. The man I was currently doing work for warned me to stay away from the small group of men that had arrived in town. "They're looking for people to impress," he told me.

"Impress?" I asked.

He gave me an impatient look. "Into the navy! They come here every so often, looking for people to force into recruitment. Now I still need you for work tomorrow, so do me a favor and try not to get noticed by them. Don't do any boat repairs today or they'll see you have some skill."

I heeded his advice. Later in the day I witnessed the press gang raid the nearby tavern. They emerged from the establishment accompanied by a couple of vagabonds that had clearly been taken against their will. One of them even tried to run.

After I finished my work that night, I bedded down in the stable. As soon as I closed my eyes to fall asleep, I heard a slight rustle come from the entrance. At first I ignored it. There were plenty of stray noises that I had grown accustomed to. But when I heard it again, this time accompanied by a soft thump, I realized a human was making the sound.

I stood up and exited the stall, only to come face to face with three heavyset men.

The only way out of the stable was past them, and for a moment surprise was on my side since they hadn't expected me to be awake. I seized the opportunity to dash between the first two and was about to sidestep the third when strong hands pulled me backward from behind. My feet left the ground as I was thrown to the ground.

I stared up at them and took in their calloused hands, stern expressions, and confident stances. These were navy men.

"How old are you, boy?" one asked unkindly.

I answered quickly and truthfully, afraid of the consequences of lying. "Eighteen."

"And your name?"

At this I hesitated, but their imposing nature prompted a response from me. "Stephen Boswell."

The one that had questioned me nodded with approval. "He'll do." Before I knew what was happening, he reached down, grabbed a handful of my shirt, and hauled me up. He kept his hand on my shoulder and walked me out of the stable, the other two close behind. When we got outside I saw a fourth man handing some coins over to the man that had employed me, the one who had tried to keep me from the press gang in the first place.

When he saw me looking at him as I was marched by, he shrugged and smiled. "At first I intervened, but... their offer was too good to pass up."

I was brought to a boat which took me to a ship, and that ship brought me to a Royal Navy port. I was grouped with many other people that had been impressed, including the two vagabonds that I had seen get taken the same day as I had. Surrounding me were beggars, drunks, thieves, merchants, deserters, foreigners, and the homeless.

Is this what my life had come to? To be sold, kidnapped, and thrown in with a bunch of criminals? Is this how the world saw me... as a criminal?

I was assigned to a ship. It was a prestigious ship, and it was huge, containing many levels below the top deck and lined with a dozen cannons on each side. The Union Jack of the British Empire flew from the top mast. I boarded it with a set of tasks to complete and several higher ranking men to punish me if I did not.

I tried to hold on to everything I believed in. I told myself that this was a good thing, that I was serving my country, that I was now furthest as I could possibly be from a life like my father's. But I didn't want to be on that ship. I didn't want to be pushed around by these officers who thought I was a nobody.

I worked dutifully. I remained respectful. I tried hard to be the best I could. Yet no matter what I did or said to myself that could make it better, or make it mean something, nothing could bring back the part of me that died the day I was impressed.

CHAPTER NINE

~ 1711, Spring ~

FOR FIVE YEARS I TOILED IN AGONY. No one was kind to me. I worked constantly. The officers scorned me. They knew I was the son of a pirate. In 1715, the navy started to actively work against piracy. Even though the ship I worked on was primarily an escort for merchant vessels or for dignitaries, that sometimes meant being called into battle with pirate ships if backup was needed or, even rarer, if the ships we were escorting got attacked. I spent these battles attached to a skilled rifleman. We operated with two rifles; while he fired off one, I reloaded the other, and then we traded to do it all over again. I would cower behind the bulwarks, my fingers shaking as I handled the weapons, trying to ignore the sounds of death around me.

It was during this time that someone from my father's pirate crew had been captured and, in order to save his own life, had given the names of the rest of his comrades. Word got around quickly, and my captain was advised that the son of Edward Boswell, first mate of the pirate ship the *Little Reckoning*, was part of his own crew.

Once the connection was made my life became even worse.

It was during my fourth year as a sailor for the navy when I met Richard Titus. I was transferred to a ship within Commodore George Madison's fleet. Despite the hate I had received from my former masters, my work ethic had been noticed. Or so a part of me hoped to believe. The other part of me thought it was the navy's way of more efficiently keeping an eye on me, now that they knew me to have "pirate blood". This ship's mission was to actively seek out pirate ships and either capture the pirates that sailed them, or, if necessary, kill them.

My commanding officer was Lieutenant Benjamin Madison, the nephew of the commodore. During a battle, as I took my place beside my assigned rifleman, Madison ordered me to help man the rigging which had come loose due to enemy chain shots. I was terrified to do anything I hadn't done before, but I obeyed.

Amidst the cannon fire, the shouting, and the screaming, I stood pulling on heavy rope to give some slack for another to tie it off, praying that this exact spot would not be hit by a cannonball. The battle raged around me and I ignored it, focusing only on this rope lest I should lose it along with the mast that it was supporting.

When the deed was mercifully done, I took a step back and seemed to truly realize what I was standing in the middle of for the first time. I cringed at it all, terribly shaken. And then I heard a loud crack and a yell and turned to see someone get flung overboard, the deck he had been standing on erupting from a cannonball, his arms flailing in the air and continuing to flail even after he had hit the water.

I felt nothing and I thought nothing. I ran the few steps it took to get to the bulwarks and then dove after him.

Under the water, the sounds of the battle became muffled. All I could hear was the splashing that Richard was making. I grabbed him under the arms and kicked vigorously to propel us up. He was a lot bigger than I was, his body built with muscle. It took some effort, but when we broke the surface both of us gasped. He kept thrashing, even as I helped him keep his head above water.

"Just calm down," I said. "I have you. Kick toward the ship. Kick!"

Somehow we made it. Richard kicked awkwardly, but our combined effort was enough to get us back to the ship. Some sailors threw a rope down. I held it out for Richard.

"No, you go first," he said. He seemed genuinely concerned about me. I almost didn't believe it.

"It's okay, I know how to stay afloat," I told him.

So he grabbed the rope and was hauled up first. The water was too violent to lie backward on, so I was forced to tread water until the rope was sent back down. As I clung to it, my already exhausted arms and legs screamed in agony. When I reached the top, hands grabbed me and pulled me over the bulwarks. And then those same hands patted me on the shoulder as I collapsed next to Richard. It was the first time I had been touched in a nonthreatening manner.

"Thank you," Richard said. He held his hand out to me. "I'm Richard Titus."

I was still wary, but took his hand anyway. "Stephen Boswell. And you're welcome."

The battle around us dissipated. I thought that would be the end of the conversation and was about to stand up, but then Richard asked, "Who taught you how to swim?"

I hesitated, both because I was surprised he was talking to me and because I didn't want to say the answer out loud. But he was looking at me with curiosity and interest and in his eyes I saw no sign of the hate or cruelty which I had learned to spot over the years.

So I answered, "My father."

And without missing a beat he said, "A pirate?"

I hung my head, gave affirmation, and scolded myself for not realizing his kindness could be too good to be true.

But then he said, "Well I'm sure glad. You saved my life." Then he chuckled. "That's never happened before. Guess I'm lucky you're here, and that your father taught you."

I couldn't believe what I was hearing. Rather, I couldn't believe that I wasn't hearing the usual harsh remarks that accompanied a conversation with me.

I pressed my luck. "You could learn, too, you know."

"Yeah?" he piped with excitement.

"Well, sure. I mean, you have the strength."

Richard chuckled. "I suppose you're right." And then his chuckle turned into a laugh. And I laughed too.

CHAPTER TEN

THE MAN ON TOP OF CAPTAIN BOSWELL pushed down on his knife with all his strength, and the captain strained to resist it as it came closer and closer to his face. A loud explosion ripped through the air as it accompanied a bullet from Titus' gun. The side of the man's head seemed to blow open, splattering blood everywhere. The man jerked then fell sideways with the momentum of the bullet.

Alice didn't bother trying to stand up. She remained crouched where she was, trembling uncontrollably, her eyes stuck staring at the dead man and the gruesome mess at his head. Captain Boswell pulled himself from under the dead man and rose with some effort, putting a hand to his face which had already started to turn deep red where he had been hit. His clothes were spattered with the dead man's blood. It made him look ominous.

"Are you okay?" he said, approaching Alice and reaching out his other hand to her. She turned away from him and hid her face in her knees. He touched her shoulder.

"No, don't!" she cried out, scrambling to get away. The captain's touch turned into a grab at her outcry. Alice twisted and screamed.

"Miss Bradford, it's okay," Captain Boswell tried to tell her, kneeling down to her level and gripping each of her arms with his hands. "Alice, it's okay! You're safe now."

Afraid to anger him, Alice calmed down. She looked at the captain and then just burst out crying. After all that, to be his prisoner again, it defeated her. Not sure how to comfort her, and not realizing that his presence was what upset her, the captain awkwardly gave her a pat. Then he stood up and offered her his hand, not forcing her to take it this time.

"Let's go back to the ship, okay?"

Alice hesitated. She imagined running away again. It was tempting, but she knew she wouldn't be able to outrun these two pirates.

She didn't take Captain Boswell's hand, but she stood up and stood next to him, waiting for him to lead the way, which he did.

Titus walked a pace or two behind them, and as they passed him, Captain Boswell muttered a thank you. Titus nodded his head but didn't say anything.

Alice didn't pay attention to the walk back. Captain Boswell could have led her anywhere. She walked beside him like a sleepwalker, unaware of her surroundings. Yet she couldn't help but look back the way they had come, longing to get away. When she did, she felt him look at her, and the glance was like a threat, making her keep her eyes locked ahead.

When the three arrived at the ship, Reuben was already there waiting for them. It was clear he wondered why they had been delayed, but he asked nothing on seeing that Alice was with them. Captain Boswell brought Alice straight to the cabin while Titus left them to tend to his duties. Before long, the *Vengeance Dragon* departed from the dock.

Captain Boswell had Alice sit on the edge of his own bed. He fetched a bowl of water and a cloth and set both items on the floor next to him while he knelt in front of her. Although he was staring at her, she didn't look at him.

"Miss Bradford, I need to tend your wound," he said quietly. Alice looked down at herself and saw that the front of her dress was covered in blood. She shuddered. Captain Boswell hesitantly lifted a hand.

"No!" Alice cried. "Don't touch me!"

"I won't. And I won't look either. I promise."

Alice relented. She let him lower the top of her dress until just the gash from the knife was exposed and nothing more. Then he took her hand and placed it at the dress's neckline so that she herself could hold it in place. He wet the cloth and pressed it against the wound.

"Ow! That hurts!"

"I'm sorry."

"It's okay," she heard herself say, surprised at the words. "Don't you have a doctor on board?"

"There's Adrian Paine, a carpenter, but all he knows how to do besides woodwork is amputation. There's also Philip Reuben, whom you've met. He has some basic knowledge."

"Well Paine has a fitting last name."

Captain Boswell let air out of his nose, like an almost-chuckle. He finished cleaning the wound and helped Alice slide her dress back up to its proper place.

"You can change into clean clothes if you'd like," he told her. "I have some that'd fit you."

Alice studied his face. He hadn't made eye contact during the entire exchange. There was a lot she wondered about him. While he had been indifferent about her presence when they first met, he now seemed to be nervous by her. The bruises on his face were now an ugly purple. Alice wondered if his actions tonight could be called a rescue if he was the one imprisoning her. If she wanted to be free, she would need to press him, but carefully.

"I don't want to be here. I want to go home." Her voice quavered.

"I know." His voice held no emotion.

"Then take me."

"I can't let you leave the ship."

"So you'll kill me?"

"No."

He looked at her. Alice's breath caught in her throat. She dared not to move, her eyes wide. Yet for the first time he didn't seem threatening or cold. Just tired, which Alice found odd. She allowed herself to relax. The captain was unpredictable. But right now, in this moment, she believed him. She also felt comfortable enough to keep the conversation going. She needed to know what he was planning.

"You've killed children before, I know it. It's their clothes you want to give me."

"I have killed children." He didn't seem bothered by admitting it. "But I won't kill you."

"Why are you doing this? What do you want from me?"

Captain Boswell didn't answer right away. "You're different. I had been intrigued by your decision to come aboard from the *Sea Maiden*, but now...." He hesitated, thinking. "I don't know. All I do know is that I want you to live."

The captain stood up. "You should rest. It'll be morning soon. I'll send Wistar to check on you." He left and closed the door behind him. He seemed to hurry out, avoiding having to answer any more questions. His words perplexed Alice. Now alone, she was glad to be rid of him. But it didn't take long for her to feel lonely. The wound in her chest wouldn't stop stinging. She wondered if she would ever be able to go home.

Alice lay back on the bed and let her head rest against the pillow. Her eyes were heavy, but she was afraid to close them.

A few hours later there was a knock at the door. Alice immediately sat up, staring at the door. She hadn't slept at all. The door crept open and Alice braced herself to see the face of Captain Boswell, but a young man walked in instead. It was the one that had first found her on the pirate vessel. The fiddler. Wistar.

"Hi," he said in a whisper.

"Hi," Alice whispered back.

"Can I come in?"

"Uh... yes."

Wistar entered. He stood beside the bed, looking down at Alice. Strangely, his presence didn't frighten her. He was fidgety, and now she could tell that he was even younger than she had first thought, in his lower twenties.

"My name's Jerome Wistar. I'm the one that found you."

"I know."

"Oh." He absently swept his hand through his messy, sandy hair. "The captain sent me to check on you."

"He said he would." There was a moment of awkward silence and then Alice finally asked, "Why are we whispering?"

Jerome grinned. "I don't know!" He covered his mouth to stifle what would have been a loud laugh and Alice found herself doing the same. "I'm Jerome Wistar."

"You already told me that!" They giggled. "I'm Alice Bradford." She offered him her hand and he shook it with cartoonish exaggeration, causing her to smile with amusement.

Alice scooted over. "You can sit if you'd like."

Jerome bowed dramatically and mocked a royal English accent. "Why, thank you, kind lady."

"That was a terrible accent," Alice said. "Does everyone on this ship speak like a colonist? You talk just like my aunt. She lives in Pennsylvania."

Jerome scratched his head. "Yes, everyone seems to. But many of us are from Britain originally."

"Are you from Britain?" Alice was hopeful.

"No, I was born in the colonies."

"How did you end up here?" Alice was genuinely curious to know.

"I had been on a ship that got attacked, just like you." He shook his head at the memory. "It's a long story."

"Really?" Alice breathed. She shifted, facing him. "Can you tell me about it? And what you did before?"

Jerome regarded her quizzically, perhaps wondering if he should discuss the topic with her. Alice watched him eagerly, and it seemed that her keen interest was apparent enough to cause him to relent. He began.

"There was this merchant ship that I had been hired to play the fiddle on. Except it wasn't really that I had been hired, more like traded." Jerome saw Alice make a quizzical face and he knew she wasn't following. "Okay, let me back up. So, before I was born, these people paid for my parents' passage to the colonies. But my parents died before they could repay the debt, so it fell on me. I was only a baby at the time. They raised me as a servant. When I was old enough to understand all this, I refused to serve them any longer. So they compromised and sent me away to the merchant ship as a musician." Jerome smiled. "They didn't like me. I didn't like them either.

"I spent years and years travelling between the colonies and Britain, entertaining the men and sending my pay back to those awful people. But then one day we were attacked by Captain Boswell's pirates. And I hid. Well they found me, of course, but only after they had already killed everyone else. Well, Captain Boswell, he offered me to join his crew. And of course I accepted because otherwise I would've been killed like the rest."

"You're a prisoner." Alice didn't ask it, she stated it.

"No, I'm not," Jerome said.

"But you are," Alice insisted. "Are you allowed to leave?"

"It's not like that. You wouldn't understand."

"Then explain it to me."

Jerome looked at her and she held his gaze. "In the colonies, I lived poorly," he said. "I had no one, and the people I stayed with weren't very kind. When I joined the merchant ship, the situation hardly improved. I wasn't treated very well and I was constantly being called on to perform. I got no rest and couldn't even keep my money. I wanted off that ship but I couldn't leave, you see?"

Jerome paused, thinking back. "When Captain Boswell gave me his offer, I thought being with pirates couldn't be worse than being on that merchant ship. And my thoughts proved true. Life is so much better. *So much better.* I get to choose when to play and when to stop. I get an equal portion of provisions earned from loot. Every man here has agreed to do their best to keep me safe. I didn't even have to sign any papers, unlike when the other crewmembers joined. This way, my name is clean. It's the captain's way of protecting me. The one condition is that I can't leave. None of us can. You see Alice, we are all bound to this ship. But none of us are prisoners here. This ship is the one place we can be free, and that's why we're here."

Alice couldn't accept it, and she told Jerome so. "Even if you don't want to leave, the fact that you can't means you aren't free, Jerome. But why is it like this? Why won't he let anyone leave? Why won't he let *me* leave?"

Jerome turned to face Alice so he could look her in the eye. "Some years ago, Captain Boswell committed some sort of crime. I don't know what it was; only a small few of the others know the details. No one talks about it much. Now, Captain Boswell is being looked for by the navy. He thinks that if anyone leaves this ship and gets caught, they'll be forced to give the navy information about him, either willingly or unwillingly. He thinks the navy will be able to find him if they get their hands on anyone who's seen him. It's his way of protecting himself. It's also why he doesn't leave any survivors anytime he takes a ship – so there'll be no one alive to be able to say that they saw him and point the navy in the right direction. He's afraid of being arrested."

"The captain is… afraid?" Alice asked.

"Well, yes," Jerome said. "In fact, he's terrified. But don't tell him I said that."

Alice could not believe what she just heard. Could it be true that Captain Boswell feared something? Could it really be?

Jerome stayed a little longer and then left Alice to rest. She was still exhausted from yesterday's trauma. She fell asleep shortly after Jerome exited the room, his former presence having caused her uneasiness to dissipate.

Alice woke up around midday. The knife wound was causing her great pain. She also felt very hot, so she threw off some of the blankets. Her throat was parched. She looked at the door, wanting to get something to drink, but it spun around her, so she decided not to get up.

Alice closed her eyes. Her body ached. She opened her eyes again when she heard someone enter the room. She couldn't make out who it was. He said something, but the voice was foggy and she couldn't decipher the words.

It's Jerome, she thought. *He's come to check on me again.*

He left rather quickly. She could hear loud voices nearby, and then two people entered. She felt a hand touch her arm and then her forehead. And then she could make out words.

"Get Paine…get Paine."

"No…" she tried to say, lifting her head. She didn't want any more pain, there was already enough.

One person left and the other stayed. He gently guided her head back down and began talking to her. She could only understand some of the words.

"Alice… thing's… okay…"

The voice was familiar. She looked at the figure but could only see a dark shadow. Then the door opened and two shadows entered so that three were now huddled around her. There was some low murmuring and then she clearly heard someone say sharply, "Touch her and you'll pay for it."

The next thing she knew, her dress was being pulled down. She helplessly started swatting at the three shadows to make them stop. Then the one with the familiar voice leaned close to her and she heard him continue talking to her until she calmed down.

There was some commotion as a fourth shadow entered. This one moved heavily and seemed to lurch at regular intervals. She heard him say in a gruff voice, "Hold… careful… me do it."

Alice's vision faded as a lot of movement ensued. She closed her eyes. This time when she opened them, there were only two shadows with her, both leaning over her: the lurching one that had been the last to enter and the one closest to her that had talked to her.

She felt something hot touch her chest. Then the heat became sharp pain as the object penetrated. Alice cried and fought weakly. The closer shadow held her still.

The object was removed after just a few seconds. She lay there whimpering. Then she closed her eyes once more.

Captain Boswell sat by Alice, holding a cool cloth to her head. Philip Reuben leaned against the wall, monitoring the knife wound as the ugly puss that had been infecting it drained away. For a moment neither of the two men spoke. Finally, Captain Boswell was the first to speak, although he kept his eyes on Alice.

"I suppose… I should say thank-"

"Don't," Reuben interrupted. The captain looked up at him, a man double his age. "There's no need for that."

"All the same…" the captain started. He was interrupted once more.

"Captain…"

"Reuben." The captain's voice was firm, final. "Thank you. If she had died… well…"

Captain Boswell looked back down. He saw her prone figure, her fragile state, her complete vulnerability. And he saw his own hand holding the cloth to her forehead.

"I don't know what I'm doing, Reuben."

Reuben thought carefully a while before speaking. "You're protecting her… are you not?" The captain's expression became troubled. Tortured, even. "It's okay, Captain. What is it about her, if I may ask?"

Captain Boswell shook his head. What was it about her? He didn't know and he didn't understand. He felt no attraction to her, no desire. He didn't, couldn't, give Reuben an answer.

Reuben said, "When you first met her, you were going to kill her." It wasn't a question.

"Yes," the captain said, pained.

"But then you changed your mind."

"Yes." It was a whisper.

Reuben tried to hide his smile. He nodded to himself and gave the captain's shoulder a pat. "Good," he muttered quietly. The captain had his eyes locked on Alice. He didn't register the pat or the word. Then, seemingly to balance precariously on his bad leg, Reuben hobbled out the door, softly closing it behind him. Once outside the bedroom, he gave in to the smile, allowing it to spread across his face, before exiting the cabin itself.

CHAPTER ELEVEN

~ 1715, Summer ~

IT WAS DURING THIS YEAR that I first gained a fascination for fencing. Long and slender, the foils used in the sport were unlike any sword I had ever seen before. I found I admired their sleekness and the strange design of their hilts. They seemed more refined than the shorter, stockier cutlasses and short swords I was used to seeing on the navy ship. Even the style used to wield them was unique. The technique called for specific foot placement. It seemed that each step and thrust had a specific purpose. Only higher ranking officers wore foils and rapiers, and only ever to flaunt their rank and importance in society. Yet of the two swords, only the foils were used in their fencing matches.

The officers had their own unique military grade sabers they carried around with them and would use in a real fight. The foils would be drawn for fencing matches when there was no immediate mission and I couldn't help but watch whenever one occurred.

An area would be cleared on the main deck to make room for the spar. Sailors would grumble under their breath as they moved away and found other tasks to perform. I, on the other hand, would stop what I was doing and find a spot to watch without being noticed.

I learned the basics of fencing just from watching the officers duel with each other. Watching carefully as they squared off, I observed their footwork, their grips, their swings. I had no way to practice on my own, lacking a sword with which to practice, someone to practice with, and, most importantly, a place to do it in secret. Hence I had no way of knowing how skilled I might be, or if what I picked up was even accurate.

Lieutenant Madison was by far the most skilled, and he seemed to know it. Despite being younger than the other officers, he would get into position with an air of almost smug confidence. Sometimes he would even smirk as he took up his stance. He also had the quickest reflexes. As soon as the duel was signaled to start, he would spring forward, immediately taking the offensive, each of his steps guiding him forward in quick succession. His opponents often didn't have time to defend themselves, or they weren't able to hold their ground and were forced backward at which point the fight would end quickly. Then Lieutenant Madison would saunter away, sometimes grinning, other times checking his sword for scratches.

He never lost a fight. Not even when he toyed with his opponent, letting the fight drag on so he could display his skill. I don't think the other officers liked being matched against him. Sometimes he would suggest a contest with rapiers to add risk of injury into the mix, but they never humored him with that idea. I couldn't help but wonder how he would fare in a real fight, or how skilled he would be if caught in a fight without his foil and instead had to rely on a cutlass or even a gun. I had never actually seen him directly involved with the pirates that we hunted. He was almost always out of harm's way, calling out orders rather than taking part in the battles.

I was supposed to be scrubbing the deck when I was finally caught watching the officers duel. I was down on all fours, the rag in my hand, my attention fixed on the fighting dance when a senior sailor came up behind me and smacked me on the head.

"What do you think you're doing?" he shouted. I quickly glanced at the officers to see if this sailor had brought their attention to my neglect of my duties. They hadn't yet, but the sailor noticed my panicked movement. "That's right, you're in deep this time."

He brought his foot back and, before I could react, the toe of his boot collided with the middle of my chest and knocked me onto my back. But that wasn't the end of it. He continued to press his foot into my chest so that I couldn't move.

I punched him in the lower leg. That was a mistake. I saw his face contort into rage. He bent down, grabbed a fistful of my shirt, and pulled me up. I defensively put my hands in front of my face and turned my head away from him, afraid to fight back again and preparing for the impact that was about to come from his fist.

"Stop!"

I slowly peeked between my hands to see his fist inches from my face. Standing a few feet away was Lieutenant Madison, foil in hand. The whole crew had gone silent, everyone watching the three of us.

"Release him," he said firmly. The sailor obeyed instantly and took a step away from me. "I will not tolerate brawls on this ship."

"Sir," the sailor said with an amount of respect that surprised me, "this pirate scum was neglecting his duties. As a senior sailor, I-"

"That's enough," the lieutenant said calmly. "I want both of you in the captain's cabin. Right now." He didn't wait for a reply. He just walked away. The rest of the crew stirred and then went back to work.

As we walked after the lieutenant, the sailor leaned into me and whispered, "Now you're really gonna get what's coming for you, pirate."

I became most scared when Lieutenant Madison held the door open for us. Once we had entered the cabin, he closed it and stood in front of it, blocking our only exit. Furthermore, the captain wasn't in the cabin, which meant the lieutenant would be able to do anything to me and get away with it. It was in that moment when I knew my life was over. He still held his sword, and I was sure he was going to use it. Next to me, the sailor smiled broadly.

"Wipe that smile off your face, Jenkins."

Jenkins, confused, looked at me, then back to the lieutenant. "Sir?"

Lieutenant Madison finally sheathed his sword. "You had no right to punish this man. An accusation must first be given to an officer, just as it has always been."

"Sir, I was just…" the sailor started to explain, but he was interrupted once again.

"Secondly, you have no right to compare any man on this ship to the criminals that we pursue." He looked at me but still addressed the sailor. "Does this man look like a pirate to you?"

"No… no, Sir," the sailor stuttered. "But, his father-"

"If his father being a pirate makes him one too, then you are nothing but a jobless, whore-loving, drunk."

I could not believe what I was hearing, let alone that it was being used in my defense, or that it was the lieutenant who was saying it, or that he was saying it so casually. The sailor was speechless. I realized I wasn't going to be killed after all.

"Now get back to work and mind your position on this ship. And I found your pistol this morning again, Jenkins. You're always leaving it around. Next time and the captain will have you flogged."

Lieutenant Madison opened the door and, without letting go of the doorknob, stepped aside to let the sailor through. I made to follow, but once the sailor had exited, the lieutenant closed the door.

He didn't look at me. He walked around me to stand in the center of the room. I waited anxiously, feeling my heart throb through my chest with nervous expectation. The lieutenant suddenly spun around to face me, drawing his sword as he turned, and pointed it at me.

I took a step back quickly. Although he kept his face neutral, I could tell he was enjoying my fright.

"So, you're interested in fencing, are you?" he said with slight derision.

"Yes, sir," I muttered, maybe a little too soon after he spoke.

Lieutenant Madison let his arm fall to his side, the point of his foil just touching the floor. It appeared to me that he was tired of this game and I was thankful.

In all seriousness he told me, "The foil is not a practical weapon on a ship. Nor is a rapier. They're too long to be used effectively with such limited space here. The foil is also too fragile in this kind of environment." With the sword still touching the wooden floor, he leaned over it, applying some weight. I could see a very visible bend in the blade. It looked like it might snap. "When the officers and I duel, we make do with the space that we have. We are forced to hold back our true skill." He paused, looking closely at me. "We also duel for sport only. There is no point in someone like you pursuing this. Do you understand?"

I nodded. Lieutenant Madison strolled right up to me. "Are you sure? Because if you don't get this sword and this sport out of your head, if you neglect your duties again, there will be consequences."

"Yes, sir," I said, my mouth dry.

He nodded to the door. I went for the doorknob, ready to run out of there like nothing else mattered. I had opened the door nearly all the way when his voice froze me.

"I'll be watching you, pirate."

I turned my head ever so slightly to look back at him, peeking out of the corner of my eye. Perhaps I feared that he would notice me looking at him. I saw his hand clenched around his sword, his knuckles white.

I didn't say anything. I dashed out of there. I went straight to my bucket of gray water, still where I had left it, got on my knees, and dug the rag across the ship's planks. My eyes stung.

CHAPTER TWELVE

A LOUD RACKET CAME FROM OUTSIDE the cabin. Titus's booming voice could clearly be heard through two doors to Alice's ears, waking her. Her head felt very heavy and her chest was sore. Touching the source of the pain, she felt a bandage there. As she sat up, she noticed that the pillow was quite damp. Then the memory of everything that had happened to her flooded her mind. She had become ill, she realized, and this dampness was from the sweat of her fever which had apparently just broke.

Alice stood. For a moment she swayed, her muscles weak and her head a bit woozy. But it passed relatively quickly. She found clean clothes and a cup of water at the end of the bed. She gulped down the water before changing and was dismayed to find that the clothes consisted of a shirt and a pair of pants. Still, even if pants were not very dignified, they were more so than a grubby dress.

She heard Titus' voice again and this time was able to make out actual words. "Quit your quarrelling, you sore losers, and either clean this up or get a proper punishment!" His yelling steadily got louder as he made his way to the cabin. "Do I look like I give a rat's ass about Griffith's cheating?!"

Alice was about to leave the bedroom when she heard the cabin door open. Instead, she decided to eavesdrop. Plus, she didn't really want Titus to talk to her, especially when he was angry.

As Titus entered, he had the last word. "To hell with the three of spades! Why don't you go ask the king of diamonds for a favor, you hapless, bum-basted idiot!"

With that, the first mate slammed the door shut.

"I can't believe these sons of-"

"Save it, Richard," Captain Boswell interrupted coolly, clearly not wanting to hear another round of pointless insults. His voice was so much quieter than Titus'. "They're really getting on your nerves, aren't they?"

In reply, Titus grumbled something incoherent. Then he asked, "Got anything to drink?" Alice didn't hear Captain Boswell answer him but soon enough she did hear the dribble of liquid being poured and knew that it was alcohol because there was nothing else to drink on the ship.

"You should have banned gambling in the Articles," Titus muttered.

Captain Boswell blew air through his nose. "And let the men die of boredom? They're just uptight because of what happened with Reed."

"Speaking of which, we need to find someone to replace Reed." A glass was set down with a loud clank. "Thanks for the drink."

"Is that all you came here for?" The captain's voice sounded amused.

"What can I say?" The door opened and closed.

Now that Titus was gone, Alice felt comfortable to leave the bedroom. She eased the door open. The first thing she noticed was two glasses sitting on the captain's desk, one empty and the other almost full with a dark liquor.

When Captain Boswell saw her, he stood quickly. "Miss Bradford. You're awake."

"How long have I…."

"A few days." He took a half step toward her, like he was about to approach her and then thought against it. "How do you feel?"

"I think I'm fine." They fell into silence.

The men's voices outside suddenly rose into shouting. Alice kept a careful eye on the captain. She saw him frown.

Seconds had hardly gone by when everything that was not secured slid to the left as the ship made a hard right. The two glasses fell off the desk and shattered on impact, liquor spilling across the floor. Captain Boswell sprang to the door. Alice, eager to know what was happening, was at his heels. Once outside, the captain collided with Titus who had already been on his way back to see him. Titus started talking before the captain could even ask any questions.

"Spanish galleon, coming from the north. They're right on us, Stephen." Titus' voice was grave. "They may have been following us since we took that Spanish trader."

Captain Boswell ran up to the quarterdeck, closely followed by Titus and Alice. The *Vengeance Dragon* had been heading south along the coast of an island but was now pointed south-west toward the inland, entering more shallow waters. The Spanish ship behind them was gaining. Isaac Owen was at the helm of the *Vengeance Dragon* and when he saw the captain he became sheepish.

"I'm sorry for the sudden turn, Captain. But that Spanish vessel just appeared over the horizon without warning and, well, it looked to me like she was trying to run us down."

Captain Boswell didn't pay heed to Owen's guilt. He simply said with respect, "Good call to turn inland. Keep her on this course. We'll lose them in the shallow water. I don't expect we'll have any trouble."

Just as the captain finished saying this, two more galleons appeared behind the first. A collective gasp rose up from the pirates of the *Vengeance Dragon*.

Alice had been standing to the side, eagerly watching on with innocent curiosity. Now she felt the mood of everyone around her change. The men became hushed and tension filled the air.

Titus interrupted the stunned silence by shouting, "Battle ready, everyone! Battle ready!" His voice bellowed across the ship and crewmembers ran off immediately to gather weapons and stow everything else while he followed them around with supervision. The master gunner, Hugh Clinton, had approached the captain for orders without needing to be called and the two conversed in quick sentences, pressured by time.

"How soon can you get the cannons ready?" Captain Boswell asked.

Clinton didn't hesitate to answer. "Immediately, sir, or close to it. But I'm not sure about the range."

"I need you to be as sure as you can. The closer we let them get, the more damage their own cannons will do to us." The captain eyeballed the three oncoming ships. "We'll try not to let it come to that, but just in case, make sure you and your men are ready."

"Aye, sir." Clinton sprinted away from the quarter deck, gathered his gunners, and disappeared below deck to where the cannons were.

Captain Boswell turned to Owen next. "Keep on the lookout for an escape. An inlet, anything. But don't enter it until we've consulted with Penn."

Having given all the orders he could, he stood and faced the enemy ships. Alice observed him. While his face revealed no emotion save concentration, she saw his hands clenched by his sides, perhaps in an effort to stop them from their barely noticeable shaking. It was subtle, but it was there, and Alice only noticed it because she had been looking for it. Was this the fear that Jerome had told her about?

"An opening, sir!" Owen called shortly, pointing to the shore. "But it's narrow. We'll have to sail up next to it before making the turn."

Captain Boswell shouted across the ship, "Penn!" Nathanial Penn, the navigator, came running. "Give me everything you can on that inlet, quick as you can. Go!"

Everything was happening so fast. Alice was intrigued by how the pirates were handling the situation. They operated smoothly despite the pressure of the threat. Yet the Spanish ships were much closer now, close enough to make out the shapes of the people aboard them. And the closer they came, the more obvious Captain Boswell's fear showed, and the more nervous the rest of the crew became.

Nonetheless, all somehow remained remarkably composed.

Penn returned quickly, having looked over his maps. "It's a safe passage, Captain. There are several routes, but sticking to the right will let us out behind them. It's too shallow for them to follow, but we can manage."

"Did you get that, Owen?" the captain asked his helmsman, who gave an affirmative.

And now Titus was relaying a message from Clinton that the cannons were ready to fire but that only half of the starboard ones would be able to make contact with their targets due to the angle of the ship. Captain Boswell said to fire anyway, yet just as he did, the leading Spanish ship fired first. It had two cannons mounted on the prow, one aimed at the *Vengeance Dragon*'s helm and one at the base of the mast.

At the thunder-like sound of the cannons, everyone on the pirate ship paused in their duties momentarily to turn their backs and cover their heads, an instinctual response to the threat of cannonballs learned over the years. Alice, however, had no such conditioning. She faced the oncoming threat with a gaping mouth, watching the two projectiles hurtle through the air. Only one thought entered her mind: This wasn't the first time she had experienced something like this.

Just before the cannonballs made contact, Captain Boswell grabbed Alice and spun around with her so quickly that her feet dangled in the air for a second. He bent over her, using his own back as a shield.

The cannonball ripped across the quarterdeck, creating a shower of splintered wood. Alice's ears burned from the sounds of destruction, as did her nose from the smell of wood dust. It was slightly off target, narrowly missing the helm's wheel and everyone near it and instead destroying only some of the stern. The second cannonball missed altogether, plopping safely into the water on the other side of the ship.

Captain Boswell released Alice and yelled, "Fire! Fire!" at no one in particular, but the order reached the right ears and the *Vengeance Dragon*'s cannons released their shots. The rest of the crew was up and recovered from the attack and had resumed what they were doing beforehand without missing a beat. Alice was the only one experiencing stunned shock at both the sudden danger that she had just survived and Captain Boswell's effort to protect her.

The *Vengeance Dragon* was now picking up speed. The inlet neared. The Spanish ships prepared to fire again, this time all three of them, and this time, having had a chance to adjust their aim, they would not miss. Aware of this, Captain Boswell frantically screamed for more speed, more speed, and it seemed that the pirate vessel had finally dominated the race and was pulling away from the enemy and turning into the inlet when the enemy fired again.

Captain Boswell jumped on the helm's wheel next to Owen, helping him to turn the ship as fast as possible. He yelled over his shoulder at Alice to hit the deck and she did so without hesitation, lying flat and putting her hands over the back of her head.

The cannons had been fired just too late to account for the *Vengeance Dragon*'s surge in speed. Those aimed at the helm passed behind the ship and caused no damage. The ship had effectively dodged them. Those aimed at the mast, however, wreaked havoc on the main deck. Alice kept her face down, but she could hear the result. The pirates sounded like boys to her as they cried and screamed in panic and pain.

The *Vengeance Dragon* passed through the opening of the inlet and sailed several more meters before losing sight of the Spanish among the tress and gaining relative safety, at least for the moment.

Now that there was nothing for the crew to do except wait, and now that the sounds of cannon fire had ceased, the *Vengeance Dragon* plunged into a would-be silence if not for the cries from the injured.

Alice slowly lifted her head. She blinked rapidly several times to clear her eyes of the smoke now that they were unprotected and propped herself onto her elbows. Captain Boswell and Owen were leaning against the helm's wheel, both breathing heavily. The captain gave Owen's shoulder a pat and a squeeze and the helmsman nodded in acknowledgement of the gesture. Then the captain pushed himself from the wheel and Owen once again took up a firm grip to continue guiding the ship through the narrow waterway.

Captain Boswell approached Alice and bent to offer her a hand. His head was turned toward the main deck, his attention fixed on his men. Alice placed her hand in his and he pulled her to her feet. Only then did he look at her, to ask if she was alright. Yet she didn't answer, for the grisly sight of the injured men stunned her.

Half a dozen were sitting or walking aimlessly with broken arms, bloodied heads, and cuts and bruises all over their bodies. One was lying prone, perhaps even unconscious. And one was writhing like a snake in a trap, screaming in utter agony. Alice felt herself go weak in the knees as she caught sight of blood and quickly looked away before she could spot the cause of it. Before anything could be said, Titus was by his captain.

"Miles has it bad, Stephen," he breathed, bereft. "Reuben and Paine can only do so much. We need a real physician."

Looking over Titus' shoulder, Captain Boswell saw the two older men attending to Miles, trying to hold him still as they tried to apply bandages to his wounds. Other men were doing the same for their comrades. Even as they tried to help, it was clear that they weren't entirely certain of what to do.

Captain Boswell let out a long breath. "We still have the Spanish to worry about."

Owen cleared his throat. "Captain, if you'd like to help with the men, Penn and I can manage over here. Between the two of us we'll be able to get the *Vengeance Dragon* to safety. We'll let you know when we're about to enter open waters again."

"Thank you, Owen." The sincerity in the captain's voice was evident, as well as the relief. He started to leave the quarterdeck with Titus and then seemed to remember Alice's presence, turning to her. "Alice, perhaps you would be more comfortable staying in the cabin."

It was a true suggestion, she realized. Not an order. Even if it had been, she found that she gladly wanted to follow it. So the three went down the quarter deck's steps together and separated at the bottom as Alice headed for the cabin. Before closing herself inside, she dared a peek back and saw Captain Boswell issuing orders to get the injured men below deck and to clear the main deck of the debris that covered it. He gave these orders while kneeling next to Miles.

Then Alice turned in and felt herself jump with surprise. The cabin was a mess! A thin layer of dust blanketed the whole room, and the bedroom in the back was littered with pieces of wood. Looking up, she was able to see through the ceiling in some areas where the cannonball had made contact.

"Well, I might as well make myself useful," she thought aloud, and set to work tidying up as best she could.

Outside, Captain Boswell had managed to calm Miles enough to keep quiet. The man occasionally let out a whimper. Man was hardly the right word, Captain Boswell thought. Miles was only twenty-four years old, one of the youngest crewmembers aboard his ship. Although Miles had grown up over the years, the captain still saw him as that sixteen year old boy who had eagerly wanted to join the crew. Miles had been a common thief. A thief who wasn't afraid to do what was necessary to keep from getting caught. That's why Captain Boswell had let him join.

Now, looking down at the bone that protruded clean from the bottom of Miles' right leg, Captain Boswell couldn't help but feel guilty for getting the boy into this situation in the first place.

"What do you think?" Captain Boswell asked Reuben and Paine under his breath. He didn't want to upset Miles with having to hear anything about the injury.

"Amputation," Paine said matter-of-factly. Captain Boswell and Reuben both stared at him, taken aback by his bluntness, and he shrugged.

Reuben shook his head. "I have to agree, unfortunately. Neither of us know how to set a bone, especially not one this bad."

Miles lifted his head shakily. "Amputate? Is that what you said?" His voice slurred as if he had been drinking too much.

"No, no, laddie," Reuben said with convincing jolliness. "You're gonna be fine. Walkin' around like me, maybe, but fine. What do you think about that, eh?"

"Oh. Yeah." Miles put his head back down and covered his eyes with his arm.

"And Doyle?" Captain Boswell asked, gesturing toward the unconscious man who was now being carefully lifted by two others.

Paine explained, "We can't say. We don't even know what's wrong with him. Hit his head, most likely."

Captain Boswell took a deep breath. "Okay. I know it's risky to move Miles, but for the sake of the rest of the men I don't want the amputation to take place up here. Bring him down and wait until we're clear of the Spanish in case we need to do any maneuvers with the ship that may mess you up. Then do what you need to do."

Captain Boswell stood and Miles caught the movement. "Alright, Captain?"

"Just need to get clear of the enemy," Captain Boswell told him gently. "Reuben and Paine will take good care of you."

Miles must have been delirious for he didn't answer right away. Then all he said was, "Alright."

The captain returned to the quarter deck. On his way he was pleased to note that most of the main deck had been cleared of its debris. At the helm, Owen told him that they were about to exit the waterway. Titus regrouped the men, putting them back on their original duties, and Clinton announced that his gunners were ready to fire the cannons if needed.

Everyone held their breath, Captain Boswell included, as the *Vengeance Dragon* left safety.

CHAPTER THIRTEEN

~ 1715, Summer ~

COMMODORE MADISON'S FLEET DOCKED regularly at the navy port. This was one aspect of being a part of the fleet that I preferred to my former ship assignment. Being on shore was the only respite I had from the constant work I was required to perform while at sea. When excused, life was very different in the harbor, especially with Titus now at my side. It was a major relief for me.

One thing always interested me each time we docked, and that was when the commodore would be greeted home by his daughter. She would wait at the edge of the dock as the ship came in and the commodore would be the first to disembark. He'd open his arms wide and she would run into them. She never failed to be there, no matter how early or late our arrival was.

The first time I saw this happen, I was enthralled. I was interested in their bond. I also wondered how their bond could last so long. She seemed to be about my age and yet I knew no one. I even found myself wishing someone would be there to greet me.

Each time this occurred, I found I was becoming more and more captivated by her. I think I mostly noticed her hair. It was long and auburn and would fly behind her as she ran towards her father. Her smile would light up her face, causing her pale blue eyes to shine.

The first time I witnessed this with Titus as my friend, he saw me looking at her and sniggered.

"Don't get too attached," he said, "and don't think you'll ever get to meet her. Commodore Madison is very protective of her. Besides, she's already engaged and soon to be married to some wealthy businessman with a foot in politics."

"What's her name?" I asked, still watching.

Richard pulled me along. "Every sailor has their fantasy, and every one learns to let it go."

"Oh, so you've eyed her as well?" I probed playfully.

"I meant everyone has had their moment of seeing her for the first time. She's the first woman that sailors of this fleet see after a long time, so they naturally fancy her for a brief period, like you now."

I didn't tell him that this wasn't my first time. "Just tell me her name, Richard."

"Alright, alright. It's Jane."

We went off, Richard leading the way, talking incessantly and I hardly listening to him as all I could think of was *Jane.*

CHAPTER FOURTEEN

THE THREE SPANISH SHIPS WERE to the south. Two were still pointed at the inlet which the *Vengeance Dragon* had used to escape. One had turned around and at the sight of the pirate vessel signaled to the other two. They began to turn around, but they were so large that they did so very widely and very slowly.

Clinton spun the helm's wheel to the left and the *Vengeance Dragon* followed suit, heading north. The island ended not too far ahead and Clinton smoothly rounded it. Now the ship was sailing west with the wind at her back.

"Full sail!" Captain Boswell called, and Titus repeated the order, "Full sail!"

The *Vengeance Dragon* picked up speed. She cut through the water like a knife, dipping and rising as she sailed through the waves. The Spanish ships quickly became dots in the distance, too heavy to match her speed and facing the wrong direction to be aided by the wind.

The *Vengeance Dragon* had been built for speed. The rush was exhilarating. Captain Boswell's hair lifted from his face in the breeze and he kept a hand on the rail in front of him. He could feel the ship come alive beneath his fingers. Clinton's gunners emerged onto the main deck, their expressions awed. It was far from anyone's first time travelling at top speed, but the experience never ceased to amaze, especially after such a close encounter with enemies.

Alice stepped out of the cabin, compelled to take a break from her cleaning and stand on the main deck the same way the gunners had. She skipped to the bulwarks and leaned over the edge to observe the water rushing by below and turned her face into the wind. Then she looked back and up at the captain and smiled with gleeful wonderment.

The amputation took place not an hour later. During that time, Reuben dressed all the injured men's wounds and got them out of the infirmary so that no one would have to be below deck during the operation. Paine repaired the holes in the main and quarter decks. He wasn't able to do much in an hour, but just enough to keep the ship from falling apart any further. Then he joined Reuben in the infirmary, saw in hand.

Before the operation began, Captain Boswell took a moment to himself. The adrenaline from the chase with the Spanish had worn off and left him feeling jittery. He needed to recover, even for just a minute, and stepped into the cabin only to find that Alice had been cleaning it and was now moving smaller pieces of furniture back to their original locations. Captain Boswell stood in the doorway, blinking.

Alice quickly straightened up, feeling that she ought to explain herself. "Oh. Well, it was quite messy in here, and then Paine came in to repair the ceiling, and well, I thought I could just…." She trailed off when she realized the captain had no interest in what she had to say. He moved toward his desk without a word and she cried out, "Watch where you're stepping!"

Captain Boswell paused mid-stride and looked down to see a neat pile of wood dust on the floor in front of him. He glanced at the opposite corner of the room and saw a similar pile of larger chunks of wood. He gave Alice a quick look of exasperation and sighed before stepping over the dust pile, reaching his desk, and plopping heavily into his chair.

"That was quite the experience today," Alice chattered. The captain's only response was to put his elbow on the desk and his forehead in his hand, slightly covering his eyes. Alice didn't take the hint. Or, perhaps she did and simply chose to ignore it. "It must be strange to be at the receiving end of an attack after spending so much time attacking others."

Captain Boswell lifted his eyes. "Can you please go bother Wistar or something?"

Alice lifted her chin in a dignified manner but complied with his request all the same. She left the cabin and closed the door softly. As the captain had mentioned Jerome to her, she couldn't think of anything else to do but seek him out. He wasn't difficult to find, sitting on the main deck and leaning against the bulwarks, his fiddle in his lap. There were several other pirates around, some sitting on the deck as Jerome was and others atop crates and barrels.

Jerome smiled as Alice approached. "Hello, Alice."

"Hello, Jerome." She sat next to him, eyeing the others carefully, but they regarded her with indifference.

"Today was terrifying," Jerome said quietly. "I'm worried about Miles." He softened his face as he looked at her. "I've been meaning to ask you how you're feeling. Since the wound and the fever, I mean."

Alice put a hand to her chest where the knife had bit her. "I've been quite sore but feeling well. Thank you, Jerome."

There was silence between the two of them before Alice finally said slowly, "I saw the fear that you had told me about in Captain Boswell. But Jerome, if he's so afraid, why do the men still follow him?"

Jerome thought a moment. "Well, it's his fear that's kept us safe for so long. Some of these men have been part of his crew for over eight years. It's rare for pirates to last that long. See, Captain Boswell will do everything to make sure he's safe, and that means everything he does will keep us safe, too."

Alice didn't appreciate that Jerome was referring to the crew as "we" and "us" rather than "them," but she didn't say so. Instead she pondered his words. Before she could get far, Jerome spoke again, and this time what he had to say actually meant something to her.

"Anyway, the fear isn't what's important. It's that he stands at the helm and faces danger despite the fear that's important. And for that he has my respect."

"You look up to him?" She couldn't keep the intrigue from creeping into her voice.

Jerome was assertive. "Absolutely."

As the amputation neared, the main deck became rather crowded. The pirates sat around, grim and silent. They all knew what was about to take place. Had the circumstances been different, Titus would have yelled at them to get off their asses and make themselves useful. Instead, aware of how they were feeling, and feeling it himself, he joined them.

Captain Boswell also joined them, emerging from his cabin. He came to stand by Jerome and Alice and leaned against the bulwarks. He looked weary.

"Wistar, strike up a tune if you would, please," he said, solemn. Jerome nodded several times and stood. His fiddle was already in his lap and so all he had to do was put it to his shoulder and draw the bow across it to start a song.

The notes that came out of Jerome's instrument were light and peaceful. Staccato mixed with long notes at the ends of lines created a distinct and memorable rhythm that the crew must have recognized for three men simultaneously burst into lyric. Jerome allowed them the first two lines before adding his own voice.

I dreamt of my beauty
And she looked down from above.
Oh, she ached in my chest
For 'tis love, 'tis love, 'tis love.

Soon the entire crew had joined in and created quite the sound. The song itself was relatively high, yet the men's voices were very deep, and the contrast was rather beautiful, especially since their thirty-odd vocals were accompanied by only one instrument.

And she said unto me,
"Fear not my dear, my beloved,
The water shall soon calm,

For 'tis love, 'tis love, 'tis love."

And smiling she left me,
Flying away with white doves.
Yet I did not cry out,
For 'tis love, 'tis love, 'tis love.

Alice clasped her hands together, moved by the music. She didn't know the words, but she joined in on the repeating line. As the lyrics came to a close, Miles let loose his first scream of pain, signaling the start of the amputation. Although the pirates cringed, they did not falter. Jerome brought them back to the top, his fiddle never slowing. Some of the men stood and all put effort into their words. Jerome pressed his bow harder against his fiddle's strings, playing louder to match the men's rising fortissimo. The resulting sound that erupted from the pirates managed to drown out the screams.

The only person who did not sing was Captain Boswell. His head was turned slightly away from the crew and he stared out beyond the ship. There was nothing but sky and water for miles in that direction, yet his eyes seemed to be locked as if something solid had been there. He was lost in his own thoughts and the music only entered his mind subconsciously. Rather than hear it, he felt it.

CHAPTER FIFTEEN

~ 1716, Spring ~

MY FATHER'S CAPTURE WAS INEVITABLE. I shouldn't have been surprised when the news reached me. But still, it shocked me. I also didn't feel as relieved as I thought I would be. I thought I would be glad to hear the news, to know that his evil ways would be put to an end. He wouldn't be able to steal or kill, to ruin innocent people's lives.

Instead I felt kind of empty. I'm not really sure. Richard asked if I was alright.

"Of course I am, why wouldn't I be?" I snapped.

"Well, he's your father, Stephen," Richard said gently. "Don't you feel anything?"

I shook my head. "He abandoned my mother and me in order to terrorize others. He's where he belongs."

My father wasn't the only pirate that had been captured. His captain and some others from his crew were with him. Our fleet changed course to England so that Commodore Madison could attend the trial. Along the way, the officers didn't pass up any opportunity to remind me of my father's fate.

When we arrived, I was told that I could attend the trial, but that I had not been called as a witness and therefore could not speak in defense of my father. I didn't want to attend and I certainly didn't want to defend him.

Richard sat with me in silence on the docked ship as we waited to hear the verdict. For some reason, I felt nervous. Eventually an officer boarded the ship and found us. He told me that my father had been sentenced to hang. The execution would take place in three days. I could visit him until then.

I spent the whole first day below deck, mostly in the dark. The ship was almost empty. Being in port gave the sailors a chance to be with their families or friends. Richard visited me as much as he could, but he also had places he wanted to go. I was the only true loner.

Richard asked why I didn't go out with him, why I didn't get out of this place. I just shrugged and said I needed to be alone.

When night came, I lit a candle and stared at its flame. I couldn't sleep. I felt like a cold hand was wrapping around me. Over and over I told myself that my father would finally pay for his crimes.

The next day, Richard convinced me to leave the ship with him. We went to a tavern where I met some of his friends. I sat slightly apart from them and did not join in their conversation. My mind was preoccupied. The cold hand had grown tighter. It sent chills across my skin.

Later, I was approached by someone who worked at the prison. He asked if I was Stephen Boswell and I confirmed that I was.

"Your father is asking to see you," he told me mechanically. "We didn't know you were here, and he didn't know either, but we found out through our navy contact. It was a coincidence, really."

I told him I would think about it. I thought about it by pacing the ship from prow to stern. I didn't want to see him. He didn't deserve to see me. I would make him wait the way he made me wait for him. These were the thoughts that went through my head. But deeper in my mind, I felt unsure and torn. Sick, even. Part of me just wanted this to end, for this all to be behind me so that I wouldn't have to think about it anymore.

Still, another part of me longed for the days when I was just a boy, living contentedly with both my parents in our little, wooden house at the outskirts of town.

Richard wanted me to go see my father. I told him there was no reason for me to go, that there was nothing my father would say that I would want to hear.

"Stephen, he's your father."

"So you keep saying."

"It's the truth."

"It's irrelevant."

He put both hands on my shoulders to make me face him. I saw his eyes dart back and forth between each of my own. I'm certain he was searching my face for answers, emotions, anything.

The truth is, I was feeling sad for my father, scared for my father, sorry for my father. I just couldn't admit it to myself or even recognize it. No matter what I tried to tell myself or convince myself, Richard was right. The man about to die was my father, and it mattered.

I woke up on the third day feeling as though sand had been stuffed down my throat. It took a lot of effort for me to actually get up, and when I finally did I ended up just wandering around the ship. At some point I found myself sitting on the bulwarks, my legs dangling over the choppy water below. I stared down, almost hypnotized, feeling the slight rocking of the ship.

A hand touched my shoulder. It belonged to Richard.

"It's happening now," he said gently.

Suddenly, I regretted everything.

"I want to see him," I gasped, almost panicky. In a rush I swung my legs over to the other side of the bulwark.

Richard squeezed my shoulder. "Stephen. It's too late."

"No!" I slapped his hand away, hopped down to the deck, took a few steps toward the gangplank. A few steps were as far as I got before Richard repeated that it was too late, causing me to falter. And then I felt an invisible rope tighten around my neck.

"Oh God… what have I done?" I sobbed, my face in my hands. I completely broke down as my shoulders shook and tears smeared my face.

CHAPTER SIXTEEN

MILES HAD GONE INTO SHOCK and Doyle had passed in his sleep, having never woken from the moment he sustained his injury. Now the *Vengeance Dragon* sailed a new kind of race; not to escape enemy ships but to find one, any one, with a doctor.

Physicians were guaranteed to be on navy ships, but to attack one would be too risky. Merchant ships would be easy to capture, but they wouldn't have a physician on board. The *Vengeance Dragon* searched for a passenger ship on which a physician could not be guaranteed, but would be likely.

Captain Boswell had Owen steer the ship toward the closest port where passenger ships were sure to be found, but to maintain distance from the port itself. Sure enough, such a ship chanced by and the pirates jumped into action.

The ship was relatively easy to take. The pirates met minimal resistance. The people on board were of the middle class. They were of no significant importance and owned no treasure, and so their risk of being attacked by pirates was low. They didn't have the means to defend themselves.

When the two ships had been anchored to each other side by side, pirates boarded the captive vessel and rounded up the passengers, fifteen in all. They had had orders to leave alive as many as possible. Captain Boswell and Titus boarded after them. Titus demanded in a loud voice that a doctor step forward. When no one moved, Captain Boswell drew his pistol and pointed it into the group at random. The people that happened to be in its line of fire cowered and tried to shield themselves with their hands.

"If you are a doctor, step forward now," Captain Boswell commanded in an icy tone. Still, no one complied. Captain Boswell opened fire. A man tumbled to the deck, blood flowing from his chest. Captain Boswell held his empty gun out to Titus who took it and replaced it with his own which was loaded. Once again the captain aimed into the group.

"Stop, please," a French-accented voice said. Captain Boswell swung the pistol to point at the man who had spoken. "Shooting him was not necessary."

"Apparently it was," the captain retorted. He jerked his gun, compelling the man to step forward. "Who are you?"

"My name is Antoine Fournier. I am a doctor."

Doctor Fournier appeared to be in his early forties, though his hair was mostly gray. He met Captain Boswell's eye with an even, steady gaze.

"Do you have supplies?" the captain asked.

"Yes."

"Gather them."

Closely followed by a pirate, Doctor Fournier retrieved his medical bag. Then Captain Boswell escorted him to the *Vengeance Dragon*, keeping the gun carefully trained on him. They went below deck to the infirmary, which was simply an area in the far corner partitioned off by curtains. Doctor Fournier took in the dead body of Doyle and the prone body of Miles in silence.

"You will save his life," Captain Boswell said coldly, "or the people you are traveling with will die."

Doctor Fournier regarded the captain with poise like a chess player whose king had just been checked. Then he turned his attention to Miles and examined his pale face, the stump of his leg, and felt the weak pulse of his heart's beat.

"What happened to him?" the doctor asked, not looking up from Miles.

"His leg was broken."

Doctor Fournier snapped his head around. "You amputated because of a broken bone?"

"It was beyond anyone here." Captain Boswell nodded toward a long shape under a blood-soaked sheet. "It's there if you want to see."

Doctor Fournier lifted the sheet. He looked at the leg for what seemed a long time. At last he turned away from it, covering it back up, and simply said, "I see." He glanced at Miles one more time and then finally faced Captain Boswell. "There is nothing I can do for him."

"Then all those people will die on your account."

"You did not listen to my words," Doctor Fournier snapped. "There is nothing I can do for him. The tourniquet was applied improperly. He has lost too much blood. The wound is already showing signs of infection. He is going to die soon. Perhaps within the hour." He softened his voice and lowered his head. "I am sorry. Please do not hurt anyone."

Captain Boswell lowered the gun slowly, staring at Miles. He felt a pressure building in his chest. A strong desire to shoot the doctor here and now crept up on him. But he pushed the feeling down, as well as the grief he was now feeling for Miles, and steeled himself.

"Then you will tend to the rest of my men. Their injuries have been bandaged, but you will be sure they are properly dressed and free from infection. Do this and no one will die."

Doctor Fournier nodded to show his compliance with the captain's terms. They walked together back onto the main deck. The captives were now sitting on the deck of their ship, and some huddled together and cried silently. The one dead man had been tossed overboard. Doctor Fournier quickly counted them to be sure no one else had been killed, and then he started talking over the bulwarks to them in French.

He was immediately surrounded by half a dozen swords and pistols and Captain Boswell warned harshly, "Hold your tongue!" Doctor Fournier shut his mouth quickly and put his hands up. "We do not tolerate foreign languages."

"I was reassuring them," the doctor explained. "They are scared. Some of them do not speak English."

"It doesn't matter. Get on with your job." Captain Boswell signaled to his men to stand down. They lowered their weapons. Doctor Fournier tentatively backed away and approached the nearest injured pirate, made obvious by the bandages covering his arm.

The men near Captain Boswell looked eagerly to him, clearly wondering about Miles' fate but hesitant to ask outright. In answer, Captain Boswell simply shook his head, and they understood, bowing their heads sorrowfully. He asked one of them, Francis Wesley, to go down and keep an eye on Miles.

As Doctor Fournier made his rounds, there was nothing to do but wait. Captain Boswell went to each of Miles' closest friends and gave them the news personally. Jerome was one such friend, yet word travelled quickly and by the time the captain reached him he had already heard. He and Alice sat side by side on the steps to the quarter deck. Captain Boswell leaned against the railing.

He sighed. "I'm sorry, Jerome. We did all we could."

Jerome nodded. "I know." He appreciated the captain's gesture at using his first name. "Is he well enough to take visitors?"

"I'm afraid not." The captain's voice was gentle. "He isn't alert and his leg is not a pleasant sight. I think it's best to remember him as he was."

They lapsed into silence and watched Doctor Fournier work as there was nothing else interesting happening on the ship. The doctor periodically glanced at Alice who squirmed uncomfortably at the attention. Captain Boswell stiffened.

When the doctor neared, he addressed Alice despite the glare coming from Captain Boswell and asked her, "Are you alright, mademoiselle?"

Alice had a hard time understanding the doctor's sentence through his accent and as she took a while to decipher what he had said, Captain Boswell answered the inquiry for her. "She's fine," he snapped. "Are you quite finished with your work?"

Doctor Fournier did his best to ignore the captain although it was clear that he was frightened. Still addressing Alice, he gave her a chance to answer, saying only, "Mademoiselle?"

"Enough," Captain Boswell snapped. "I told you she's fine." He took a threatening step forward and the doctor backed up to maintain the distance between them.

Doctor Fournier stood defensively. He seemed to be gathering his courage. And then he said, "I would like to hear it directly from her."

Jerome stood suddenly. Tension filled the air, but not just from Captain Boswell and Doctor Fournier, but from two of the other pirates who had overheard the dialogue so far. Alice didn't understand what the big deal was. She had assumed that the French doctor was interested in knowing if she had injuries that he could tend as he had done for the men. Not wanting the situation to escalate, Alice started to say that she *was* fine, but Captain Boswell sharply cut her off with, "Don't answer him, Alice. He is making poor assumptions and sticking his nose where it doesn't belong."

Doctor Fournier carefully interpreted those words before trying once more to get a straight answer. "Mademoiselle, why are you on this ship?"

Alice kept her mouth closed, both in obedience to the captain's request that she not satisfy the doctor's query, and due to her shock at the aggressiveness with which the pirates reacted to the doctor's question. The first two pirates now approached and three others that were farther away turned their attention over.

"Leave her alone," one of the closer ones warned, and Alice saw it was Hugh Clinton, the master gunner, who spoke. She wondered why he was defending her when they had never talked to each other before, or even formally met. She also wondered what exactly it was he was defending her from. Doctor Fournier seemed sincerely concerned about her and she didn't get how that would cause the pirates unease.

The standoff was frightening. Doctor Fournier stood boldly, holding eye contact with Captain Boswell. Captain Boswell stared at him coldly.

Reuben's voice came as a growl from across the ship. "Don't do anything rash."

Neither man spoke. They both seemed to be taking Reuben's advice. Yet before anything else could develop, Francis Wesley ran up to the deck from the infirmary, his eyes wide and hands shaking, and announced in a broken voice, "Miles... Miles just went. He's gone."

The pirates reacted to the news with a wide array of emotions. Some that had been standing now slumped down as Jerome did, distraught. Others stood, seething with anger. Still, others shook their heads, pitying the loss.

Captain Boswell addressed Doctor Fournier carefully through a clenched jaw. "Are you done seeing to the men?" The doctor gave a curt nod. "Go back to your ship. You're leaving." To the pirates he said, "Help them leave."

Doctor Fournier obeyed. Yet as he walked toward his ship and his companions, he became wary as he realized he was being followed. He stopped when he saw the pirates that were guarding his companions were readying their weapons.

"What are you doing?" he cried. He was roughly grabbed and forced to keep moving. The first shots rang out and he filled with horror as he saw some of his companions drop, dead. He struggled against the men that were holding onto him. "No! Stop!"

The passengers screamed and some tried to run although there was nowhere for them to go. Swords and guns alike took them down. Doctor Fournier's knees went weak. His face was soaked in tears and sweat. Captain Boswell walked up to him. He held his own pistol again, now reloaded.

"Why are you doing this?" Doctor Fournier gasped between sobs.

"You didn't save Miles. That was the deal."

"But there was nothing I-"

Captain Boswell fired and the doctor went silent. As he sagged sideways, one pirate supported his shoulders and the other took his legs. They lifted him up like a sack in one fluid, practiced motion and tossed him over the bulwarks onto his own ship.

Captain Boswell walked away. He left his men to take care of the ship, confident in their ability to sink it without leaving a trace that it had ever been there. He hadn't gotten far when he was stopped by Alice. She stood right in his path, her arms crossed over her chest.

The captain stepped around her, obviously irritated. "I'm not in the mood to hear what you have to say about me."

Alice spun slowly so that she continued to face him even as he moved around her. She let her arms fall by her side. "I was going to ask how you came to be like this."

Captain Boswell just shook his head and continued on, never slowing.

After the *Vengeance Dragon* had pulled well away from the French passenger ship and left the vicinity of the port, the bodies of Doyle and Miles were weighted and wrapped up in sheets and laid on the main deck. The entire crew was assembled around them. Titus gave some words about each man, about how they were dutiful and brave. He joked about Doyle's Irish descent and Miles' habit of playing pranks on the other crewmembers. Then, one at a time, each body was gently lowered over the side of the ship into the water below. The proceedings were accompanied by Jerome on the fiddle.

The men lined the side of the ship, leaning over it and watching the two bodies disappear into the dark depths of the ocean.

The following days were filled with a sense of mourning. The crewmembers were not their usual talkative selves. It seemed a dark cloud had cast itself over the *Vengeance Dragon*.

It only took a few weeks for that cloud to become literal.

In the far distance, a storm was rolling across the sky. The entire crew stared at it in silence, filled with apprehension. It was only a matter of time before the mass reached the *Vengeance Dragon* and unleashed its storm upon all of them.

"We can't outrun that," Owen said, dread in his voice.

Captain Boswell crossed his arms. "No."

Alice felt a knot form in her stomach. The men scurried around, securing everything, stowing their belongings, and closing the hatches. They did all this at record speed, like their lives depended on it, and that's what scared Alice the most.

CHAPTER SEVENTEEN

~ 1716, Spring ~

I CAME TO HATE EACH AND every one of the sailors on this navy ship. All but Richard. Later in the same day that my father was executed, some of the crew returned to the ship to give me the official news of his death. Only one of them actually held the task. The others tagged along to see how I would react.

Before they arrived, I confessed my regrets to Richard through painful sobs. We sat on the steps to the quarterdeck and he gave me an occasional awkward pat on the back.

"I did care about him," I told him, "but I didn't want to. He's all I had left, and now he's gone, and I didn't even get to say goodbye, or that I forgive him, which I think I do now." It all poured out of me. "And even if I didn't care about him I should have let him see me because I know he has always cared about me. Also… there were some things he told me and I… I've been thinking about them."

"What things?" Richard pressed.

"Things about the people above us. In class, I mean, and rank." I hesitated. "Only, I'm not sure what to think. My father was a pirate and piracy comes with consequences. The navy was just trying to protect innocent people."

"I don't understand what you're talking about," Richard admitted, although I could hear a ponder in his voice.

That was when the crew arrived. They hung back just a bit as the messenger approached. Richard and I stood up. He didn't speak for a few seconds. He looked at me a little too closely for comfort. I was nervous.

"Edward Boswell is dead," he stated at last with no emotion. "After a minute of kicking his hands came loose from their bonding, but just as he started reaching for the noose he lost consciousness." A grin crept onto the man's face.

"That's enough," Richard snapped.

"After five minutes, the crowd assumed him to be dead and threw spoiled food at his body, trying to keep the show going."

The man continued to recount the event in vivid description, giving me a picture that I didn't want to see. He threw in jokes here and there, getting the crew to laugh. Richard tried to get them to shut up but then they teased him and accused him of only being my friend so that I could repay him "intimately."

I saw the scaffold. I saw my father standing on it. I saw him get hoisted into the air. I saw the life leave him. My blood boiled. When previously I may have been crying out of sorrow, now my eyes stung with hate.

I stepped forward, drew back a fist, and punched the man right in the middle of the face. He toppled backward, his nose broken, his lip split.

Everyone went silent. They stared at me in awe. But then I saw their eyes shift toward the gangplank and their expressions turn to mockery. And one man gave the call that froze the blood in my veins, "Commodore on deck!" I followed their gaze. The commodore, captain, and lieutenant were standing several paces away and it was clear that they had seen my act of violence. Everyone snapped to attention. And so did I, although I knew doing so wouldn't save me.

The captain and lieutenant both looked at the commodore, clearly waiting for him to issue an order. But he looked to the captain and said with a shrug, "It's your ship." The captain, in turn, looked to the lieutenant and muttered, "You've spoken to him before."

The lieutenant looked at me. "So I have." He addressed those present but still kept his eyes locked on mine. "Seize him."

Two sailors jumped forward, eager for the chance to grab my arms and hold me between them. Richard looked as though he was going to intervene and I whispered, "Don't do anything stupid." He backed away and I felt relieved.

The lieutenant helped the man I had punched to his feet and even offered him his own handkerchief to wipe the blood dripping from his face. That's when it first hit me how serious my offence actually was.

"Striking a fellow sailor is forbidden," Lieutenant Madison announced. "Stephen Boswell, you are guilty of this offence and will suffer two dozen lashes to the back as punishment." To the man I had hit he said, "Woods, you may carry out the punishment if you choose as recompense for your injury."

My heart sank and my legs went numb. I had never committed a serious crime before, and rarely even a minor one. I had tried to never make a mistake that would give the navy any cause to punish me. And here I was, about to be flogged, for committing a crime of my own purposeful will.

The shirt was stripped from my body. My arms were extended outward and tied at the wrist to one of the shrouds that held in place the mast, my bare back facing the inside of the ship. I heard more of the crew arrive. Word of the ensuing punishment travelled fast. Out at sea it was mandatory for the crew to attend a punishment. Here in port, most arrived out of interest in seeing me suffer. The pirate son whose father was just hanged that same day.

I had seen many floggings take place. I knew that the crew had now assembled in a half circle around me. The captain would retrieve the cat-o'-nine, a whip made of nine rawhide lashes, each knotted at the end. He would hand it to Woods, the man I had struck.

I could not see any of these proceedings. All I could see were other ships docked nearby and the ocean stretching out beyond them. I tried to focus on this beautiful sight. I tried to imagine that I was a child sitting on a rocky shore with my father, throwing stones into the water. I tried to breathe calmly, to match the rhythm of the waves.

Despite my efforts, I breathed in a panic, my chest heaving up and down. I shivered uncontrollably, both from cold and from fear, and my lip trembled. My mouth was bone dry and though I tried to moisten it by moving my tongue around within, I found that my nerves had even taken over that muscle. I waited in terror for it to begin.

The first lash came rather suddenly. Nine cords bit into my flesh at once and tore downward across my back. I cried out immediately in shock and pain, pulling unintentionally against my restraints. Nothing could have prepared me for this agony. Hardly any time had gone by before the whip attacked me again, this time digging into my back much deeper. I even heard a grunt of effort come from the man doing this to me as he struggled to put as much strength into the blow as he could.

The third strike killed any bravery that may have still been inside of me. I had seen men stand where I now stood, with firm footing and back straight, make not a sound or a movement as they took their punishment. I had seen other men who leaned either forward or backward, perhaps in an effort to lessen the pain, grunt or gasp with every lick of the whip. When the third strike came, I screamed and writhed, flashes of bright color bursting in front of my eyes.

At one point my back went completely numb. With each strike I could only feel a sharp sting and a force that pressed me forward. The sensation of my own hot blood running down my body was foreign to me, and for a second I even wondered what it was, the realization making me feel dizzy with nausea. However, this feeling only lasted until the next blow struck me, which caused my knees to collapse from fatigue.

The interval between each lash started to grow in length until the whipping ceased altogether. The sense of relief that I felt was astounding. I allowed myself to take in large gasps of air but was too weak to regain my footing, and so let my restraints hold me up. I could hear words being exchanged behind me but a cloudiness in my ears only let me hear muffled voices. I could not discern anything that was being said, but frankly I did not care.

Then all at once the nine cords scourged me again. The whip attacked with renewed energy and with a new, quicker speed. I wished I could black out. Or even die. But it ended quickly. One, two, three, four. And it was over just like that.

Even as I was untied, part of me was afraid to believe that it was truly over. Richard would tell me hours later that after twenty lashes, Woods no longer wanted to continue whipping me. So the captain had excused him and taken up the whip himself to finish the sentence.

When I had been released from my bonds, I dropped like a marionette that's strings had been cut, and I sank into a pool of my own blood. I had to be carried away. Below deck, as tears streamed from my eyes, salt was rubbed into my new wounds.

It seemed that an eternity went by before I could finally breathe normally again. Richard sat by me as I lay on my stomach, bandages covering my back. We were alone, as we had been when this day had started.

"It's over, Stephen," Richard said, trying to reassure me. "You can relax now. Everything's going to be okay."

I closed my eyes, too tired to keep them open. Richard stayed a little longer and then I heard him leave. Although I tried to relax I couldn't. I had suffered a trauma that never had and never would be paralleled. Despite Richard's words, everything was not okay.

CHAPTER EIGHTEEN

IT ONLY TOOK HALF AN HOUR before the storm caught up to the *Vengeance Dragon*. As the wind picked up, the sea began thrashing violently against the hull of the ship. The entire sky had gone black and released a torrent of rain.

Captain Boswell grabbed Jerome's arm. "Take Alice into the cabin and make sure she stays there. This is going to be a dangerous storm. Do you understand?"

"Yes, Sir."

Jerome did as he was told. He took Alice's hand and they ran to the cabin. It took some wrestling to get the door closed behind them.

They stared at each other. Then the cabin lit up as lightning streaked across the sky outside accompanied by a violent clap of thunder. Alice could feel the sound in her chest and the floor shake beneath her feet. Jerome opened his mouth to reassure her, but at that moment the ship listed so far to one side that they both fell over. Some of the captain's papers scattered across the floor.

"Just what do they think they're doing out there?" Alice asked, her voiced raised, as much to be heard as out of panic. "They can't fight the weather!"

"No, they're trying to keep the ship from sinking." Jerome sat next to Alice against the wall in the corner.

"We could sink?" The fear in the girl's voice was evident.

"Surely not. Captain Boswell knows what he's doing, and so do the men. This isn't the first storm we've been through."

Alice knew Jerome was just trying to make her feel better. She could tell that he was worried. The ship continued to lurch violently, but on the floor the two were relatively safe from injury.

It soon became pitch black. Alice could barely see Jerome sitting next to her. Her muscles were tense and this caused her body to tire and ache. The storm had not let up, yet her initial fright had waned.

Outside, waves were crashing over the side of the ship. Men hurried to and fro with buckets, desperately tossing the water back into the ocean before it could build up and weigh the ship down. Others cared for the ropes and shrouds that held up the mast, looking for weak spots caused by the water and reinforcing them or tying whole new knots.

Captain Boswell stood by Owen at the helm who was trying to keep the wheel as steady as possible. They took turns every so often. The wheel was like a bucking bull and to hold it for any amount of time quickly tired out the arms.

The rain pelted the captain's back and sent shivers up his spine, but he paid it no heed, keeping his attention focused on the task at hand. The rain also made it difficult for him to see for the only way to keep the water out of his eyes was to either keep his head down or to blink rapidly.

An exceptionally large wave approached the port side. The *Vengeance Dragon* dipped down before it as it grew ominously.

"Brace!" Captain Boswell shouted. The wind took his voice. The wave crashed down, knocking some men off their feet. The captain saw one of the ropes that they had been looking after start to snap, its threads giving way one at a time.

Someone else saw it, too. Adam Paisley, a gunner, ran from the other side of the ship. He reached his hand out and caught it just as it separated. The sudden tension that it released sent a jolt through Paisley's shoulder, but he held on fast. The others regained their feet and quickly aided him in reattaching the rope with a strong knot.

Captain Boswell let out a breath he hadn't realized he was holding.

Inside, Alice and Jerome tried to talk, but between the thunderous pounding of the rain and the thunder itself, they couldn't hear each other very well. They huddled together. Jerome clutched Alice with one hand and his fiddle with the other. They had no idea how much time was passing. It felt like hours. Eventually, Alice fell asleep with her head against Jerome's arm.

In the early morning, blinding, bright light flowed into the cabin through the window. Alice's eyes had already been closed from sleep, and she found it easier to keep them closed. She lifted a hand to create some shade. Her movement stirred Jerome.

"The storm broke!" he said with excitement and relief. He stood up slowly and winced at the cramps in his joints. Even though the ship was no longer pitching, he had to steady himself with a hand on the wall.

He offered a hand to Alice and helped her up. She stretched, feeling the kinks in her body loosen and slack. Her neck was sore and she rubbed it.

They could hear a lot of movement and talking outside. It seemed that the men hadn't had a rest yet. A moment later, Captain Boswell entered the cabin. He was soaked through with rainwater, his dark hair matted to his forehead and water dripping from the bottom of his frockcoat. He shook it off and threw it haphazardly over the back of his chair.

"Are you two okay?" he asked. His voice was hoarse.

"Yes, Sir, we're fine," Jerome answered. "And you? And the men?"

Captain Boswell went to his drink cabinet and started pulling all the full bottles of various liquors that he had never drank, tucking them under both arms in order to carry as many as possible.

"There's still work to be done," he said, not directly answering the question. "If you have a mind to play I would greatly appreciate it, Wistar."

"Of course." Jerome even sounded eager to do so. Without a word, he and Alice took each other's hands. Captain Boswell noted the physical contact, only slightly surprised at it. All three of them exited the cabin together.

The storm had made quite a mess of the ship. The deck itself was sodden. The crew seemed greatly disorganized as they made repairs, cleaned up, and expelled water from the hold. Alice had never seen them like this before. They were taking time to sleep in shifts, and those that were awake now portrayed pure exhaustion.

As Jerome started to play a cheery tune, Captain Boswell distributed his drinks among his men. The kind gesture alone seemed to give them drive. Then the captain went to work alongside them.

It took most of the day for all the work to be done. The bright sun helped to dry the wood of the ship. Captain Boswell did not return to his cabin, not even once, until everything was finished. He had gone the longest without sleep, over twenty-four hours, and as the work came to an end, it started to show. Alice couldn't help but feel concern for him. When he finally turned in, she followed, although she couldn't have said why.

Captain Boswell staggered inside, his steps heavy. His papers were still on the floor but he didn't seem to notice. He put his hands on the edge of his desk and leaned forward against it, his head bowed.

"Captain… are you alright?" Alice asked tentatively.

He squeezed his eyes shut for a moment and then pulled them open again with some effort. He glanced at his chair. Then at the bed in the back. "Miss Bradford. May I use the bed?"

"Don't be daft!" Alice exclaimed. "Of course you can use it!"

"Thank you," he breathed. He pushed himself away from the desk and made his way to the bedroom. He dropped onto the bed, not even bothering to close the door, and shut his eyes immediately.

"Don't sleep in damp clothes. You'll catch a cold!"

He said something inaudible. Alice had never heard him mumble before.

"Captain?"

Deep breathing was his only response. Alice quietly closed the bedroom door. She picked up the papers from the floor and set them neatly on the desk. Then she took the captain's coat and brought it outside, draping it over the bulwarks to dry. Out here, terrible screeches from Jerome's fiddle met her ears. She looked over to see that Francis Wesley was playing the instrument while Jerome looked on and laughed at his lack of skill.

Someone approached Alice and she stiffened, seeing a large figure out of the corner of her eye. It was Titus. She didn't look at him.

"You seem to be doing well," Titus spoke. It sounded like a growl. "All recovered from your little injury?"

Alice tried to be polite and not let her discomfort show. "Yes, thank you."

Titus snorted. "Ah, don't thank me. It was the captain who did all that." He let sarcasm slip into his voice. "You know, first he takes a beating for ya, then he conquers that little infection. Don't know what's gotten into him. Don't know why he's suddenly so keen on keeping you alive." He leaned over her. Alice could smell strong alcohol on his breath. She nervously shifted her eyes back and forth between his face and the deck, wanting to hold eye contact but finding it difficult to do so.

"Well, I'm grateful to him," Alice said, hoping to end the conversation.

"Ha!" Alice jumped at his outburst. "Are you now?" He pointed a finger at her. "You remember what he's done to you, don't you? What he's done to your father? Grateful? Ha!"

Alice felt herself start shaking all over. She thought she might be sick. Should she walk away without a word? Or would that only instigate Titus more?

"That's enough." Reuben's gruff voice cut through Titus' laughter, if laughter is what you could call his insensitive guffaws. "Why don't you go get some sleep, Richard, eh? I think you might be delirious."

"Sure, sure," Titus muttered, making light of the confrontation. He walked off and briefly yelled at Francis Wesley to cut out the blasted racket he was making with Jerome's fiddle.

"Thank you, Mister Reuben," Alice said sincerely, turning to the older man.

Reuben smiled. "Oh, there's no need for that, little lady. How are you holding up?"

"I'm quite alright. Last night was scary. But Jerome was with me."

"Yes, he's rather fond of you."

Alice looked across at Jerome. "Is he?"

Reuben chuckled. "As a matter of fact, I believe 'sister' was the word he used when last we spoke." Alice smiled, feeling gratified. Reuben continued in a more serious tone, "He's not a pirate. I know you don't want to be here, and I'm sorry that you are. I am. But know that you aren't alone."

Alice's smile faded. She wasn't sure what to make of those sentences. Reuben sensed her discomfort. He changed the subject mercifully.

"Is this the captain's coat?" he asked, noticing it for the first time and touching it briefly.

"Yes, it was soaked all the way through and I brought it out to dry. Captain Boswell just threw it over his chair, dripping and all." Alice huffed. "And now he's sleeping in damp clothes."

"Well, he's had a long night and a long day." Reuben patted the bulwarks. "And so has the *Vengeance Dragon.* We'll have to bring her to shore, clean her underside and make repairs."

"Seriously?"

"Careening, we call it. We'll be quite exposed, but it's a necessary risk." Reuben breathed in deeply and formed his next words as he exhaled. "Well, I'd better get to cooking. Thinking of making something real special for tonight."

"Thank you for talking with me, Mister Reuben," Alice said.

"Anytime, little lady." Reuben walked off, smiling as always.

As the day came to a close, Captain Boswell still slept. Reuben visited him, bringing food and gently putting a hand to his forehead to check for fever, before turning in himself. Most of the crew also slept. The shifts of their regular day to day routine had become disconcerted and it wasn't until the next morning that their routine was reestablished. With nowhere else to spend the night comfortably, Alice spent it below deck with the men, but only after she had returned the captain's coat to the cabin. She was wary of them, but they hardly even looked at her. A few even offered her brief, polite greetings. She recognized Isaac Owen and Hugh Clinton as two such men.

Alice stayed in Jerome and Francis' nook of the sleeping quarters. There were beds, bunks, and hammocks. They gave her a top bunk. The men gathered in groups based on their roles. At this end were the sailors, at another were the gunners, and in the middle were the officers. The night watch went above, hardly interacting with anyone else.

They told each other silly stories. Alice gained the attention of some crewmembers as she recounted how her aunt in Pennsylvania never failed to hang a British flag outside her house anytime British soldiers were in town, but would always say nasty things behind their backs which instigated arguments with her brother, Alice's father.

The crew clapped and laughed at her story. It made Alice feel content. Some of the men at the other end of the sleeping quarters seemed displeased. The crew was divided by her presence, she realized. And not just down here, but on the ship in general.

When the lights were put out, Jerome and Francis bid Alice good night. She tucked herself into bed and slept soundly, comforted by the snores of those closest to her.

The next morning, Alice rose before most of the men, already having been rested from the night before. She silently crept up to the main deck so as not to wake any of them and made her way to the cabin. She was pleased to see that Captain Boswell was awake and had changed into fresh clothes.

"Miss Bradford," he said with slight surprise at seeing her enter. His voice was scratchy and he let out a brief cough.

"Good morning, Captain." She smirked. "You wouldn't be coughing if you had changed your clothes before sleeping."

He glanced at his coat now draped neatly over his chair, as well as the papers on his desk. "Did you move these?"

"Why, yes," Alice admitted, a little embarrassed. She didn't offer any explanation and it didn't seem that Captain Boswell was looking for one.

"Where did you sleep last night?"

"Oh, below with the men."

Captain Boswell snapped his head up. "What!"

"Yes, they were very kind. Although, I think some don't like me. Oh, but they enjoyed the story about my aunt from Pennsylvania."

Captain Boswell ran a hand through his hair. He seemed frustrated at receiving all this information at once, and that Alice was giving it to him in such a chipper tone as he had never heard from her before.

Then Alice thought back to her conversation with Titus with apprehension. He had given her two sides of Captain Boswell so plainly and cruelly. Yet was not one as true as the other? The captain had stolen her life away... but he had also saved it, and on more than one occasion.

"Captain..." she started slowly, timidly, "I've never thanked you for... for before... and I think I ought to. So...."

Captain Boswell put up a hand, silencing her. Then he lowered it and stared at her with what appeared to be concern.

"You don't need to do that." His voice was firm, but it was also gentle, the first time that Alice had heard it like that. "That's not a position I want to put you in."

Alice nodded her acceptance of that statement. For the first time, she felt that he understood exactly what he had been putting her through all this time. An unspoken acknowledgement passed between them.

CHAPTER NINETEEN

~ 1716, Spring ~

M Y BACK WAS SORE FOR SEVERAL WEEKS, but the
pain subsided within a few days. I was back at
work quicker than I thought I would be.

I was always on edge. If an officer or a senior sailor ever
walked by me, I would tense up unintentionally. If they
spoke to me, I stood ready to defend myself, fearing that
they were going to attack me. Of course, they never did.
But at the time I couldn't help thinking that everyone on
that ship was plotting to harm or kill me.

And then one day as I emerged onto the deck as we were
docked in port, I looked to the shore and saw Richard
talking to Jane, the commodore's daughter. My breath

caught in my throat when I saw her. She was beautiful, as always.

I walked down the gangplank and approached the two. When Richard saw me coming, he seemed to become embarrassed, but only for a second.

"Miss Madison," he said all gentleman-like, "this is Stephen Boswell. Stephen, this is Miss Madison."

She turned to face me, her eyes bright and her mouth formed in a full smile. She gave me her hand. "A pleasure, Stephen. Please, call me Jane."

I awkwardly took her hand, having never been introduced to a lady before, and said, "Hello." Her hair was a soft brown, though when picking up the sunlight I could see a tinge of orange. It cascaded around her face and fell past her shoulders, curling at the tips. Her hand was small compared to mine and felt so delicate. The skin was soft and light and I had never felt anything like it.

It took some effort to pull my eyes from her allure and look at Richard with a question in my eyes, asking him to explain himself.

He cleared his throat. "We haven't met before. I mean, we just met."

"I saw Richard over here and figured I'd come talk. I've never had a proper conversation with a sailor before." She said all this with obliviousness to our awkwardness. I also couldn't help but notice that she looked at me as she spoke. "So you sail with my cousin too?"

It took me a moment to understand her question. "Uh, yes, Lieutenant Madison."

"He sure loves his title," Jane muttered. "Tell me what it's like to be a sailor. It's amazing, I'd imagine. Like an adventure!" Her eyes sparkled.

I didn't have the heart to tell her the truth about my experiences, about how most of the time I was enduring a living hell. So I just told her that being a sailor was fine, although I could no longer look at her. Richard took my resulting silence as an opportunity to recall all the heroic deeds he had done, most of them exaggerated.

Yet even as he spoke, Jane continued to watch me. She respectfully made eye contact with Richard once in a while, but it was on me that her true attention was focused.

After a while she very lightly touched my arm and I jumped. We both immediately said sorry to each other.

"Are you okay?" she asked, and she seemed genuinely concerned.

I stuttered with my words. "Yes, I just, I'm, well…." At that moment I saw the commodore enter the port, clearly looking for someone. I assumed he was looking for his daughter. "I should go, actually."

She noticed the commodore as well. "Don't think you have to go because of him."

I took some steps backward. "It's… it's much more complicated than you think."

"Wait, Stephen." I stopped and waited, staring at the ground before her feet. "Well, I'm glad to have met you and I hope we can meet again."

I nodded slowly, and even let a smile creep onto my face. Then I hurried back onto the ship. From there I saw Commodore Madison join Jane and Richard. They conversed a bit, and then Jane and her father exited the port. Richard came to me then.

I punched him in the arm and grinned. "How did you manage to meet her?"

"I don't know, it was like she said. I was just standing over there and she came to me."

"Well, you're one lucky lad, Richard."

"Me, the lucky one?" He shook his head. "She seemed more interested in you, Stephen."

I think logically I knew he was right, but I just couldn't believe him. I felt I was in a daze.

"Well what happened when Commodore Madison came?"

He shrugged. "Just some small talk." He hesitated. "You came up and, uh, Jane found out about your father. Sorry, Stephen."

All I could say was, "Yeah."

I thought that would be the last I would see of Jane. Although I was disappointed, I didn't let it bother me. I resigned that we would never be able to be friends.

Except that wasn't the last I saw of her. Hardly a day had gone by when I saw her standing in the same place that I had just met her. I aimed to walk by her quickly, before she could notice me. But it turned out she had been waiting for me and called my name as soon as I was within earshot.

I don't know what I was expecting her to say. I'm sure I thought that whatever it was, it wasn't going to be positive. When I approached her, I immediately noticed that her eyes were sad. To me, this was confirmation of my suspicion.

Yet when I stopped a few paces away from her, she closed the gap, her hands clasped in front of her. "Stephen. They told me about your father yesterday. And I wanted to say that I'm so sorry."

I assumed that she was referring to the fact that my father had been a pirate, or at least something along those lines, especially after what Richard had told me about her finding out. So I shrugged and muttered something about how it was the life he chose.

Jane leaned forward. "No, I'm sorry that he passed away. It must have been hard to lose him."

An enormous wave of sorrow swelled up in me. I hadn't really thought about my father's death much, or at least tried not to. However, as quickly as the sorrow came, it was replaced suddenly by defensiveness.

"He got what was coming for him," I snapped.

Apparently, Jane didn't believe that I really thought that. She also ignored my comment. "I'm sorry. Stephen."

I looked at her. I saw sincerity. I saw sympathy. It had been weeks since my father was executed. No one had given me what Jane now gave to me. I covered my eyes with a hand. No tears came, as they might have before. After that day, they were all dried up now. Yet I could not speak.

Then I felt her hands touch my shoulders. They slid around to my back and pressed me to her. She held me in this embrace for a moment and I felt like a frightened child. But I also felt safe. And I felt for the first time in a long time that someone in this world truly cared about me.

"I don't care what my father might say about you," she said. "You can talk to me, if you like, any time." She released me. "I mean it."

"Thank you." My voice caught on the words.

Richard was waiting for me and I told Jane I needed to go. She made me promise that we would speak to each other the next chance we got.

When I met up with Richard, he asked what Jane and I had talked about. The question caught me off guard a bit, but I brushed it off. I figured he had seen us from a distance as he went to the place at which we had agreed to meet. I thought he would be impressed, but he remained stoic. The matter never came up again.

CHAPTER TWENTY

ALICE STOOD IN THE PROW of the *Vengeance Dragon*, eagerly watching as the shoreline appeared in the distance. The island was inhabited by a tribe of natives who had made a pact with Captain Boswell, allowing him to beach his ship on their land in exchange for firearms and gunpowder. They would be able to warn the crew of any enemy presence, and each had agreed to help defend the other if the need were to arise.

It was obvious that Captain Boswell was nervous. Although repairing and cleaning the bottom of the ship was essential, he feared the idea of having no escape should something go wrong. In fact, the ship was overdue for the procedure, and Titus had to remind his friend that they would be no better off if the hull suddenly splintered while they were sailing, or if the ship was unable to reach its top speed during a chase. The men prepared all day long, bolting down some supplies while moving others. Alice helped, too, by stowing the little belongings she had within her bedroom.

Yes, *her* bedroom. In the time it had taken to reach the island, Paine had completely renovated the cabin at the behest of the captain who had clearly been bothered by Alice's one night with the men. The one bedroom had been split into two and each extended out a little, decreasing the size of the main room. Alice had her own private nook now, complete with a simple bed and a chest for storage.

As the ship approached the island, Isaac Owen judged the distance with a careful eye and then signaled for the anchor to be dropped. The *Vengeance Dragon* came to a full stop, bobbing up and down. The men lowered a small rowboat stashed with guns over the side of the ship and Captain Boswell along with a few others climbed down into it. Alice watched with intrigue as the small party went to shore and were greeted by a group of dark-skinned natives. The natives, despite their simple outfits and strange piercings and tattoos, were armed with modern rifles.

Captain Boswell shook the hand of one native and clapped arms with another. He seemed to get along well with them. After a bit of talking, the guns were removed from the rowboat and half of the natives carried them away from the beach and into the dense jungle toward their tribe. Then Captain Boswell beckoned to the *Vengeance Dragon*. The anchor was raised and the ship floated up the beach, grinding against the sand beneath it. The men already on shore helped guide it.

"Alright!" Titus bellowed, rubbing his hands together. "We got a little over six hours to get this done, so let's get to it!"

Alice stood there, more than a little confused. Sure, the ship was now aground, but she thought the whole point had been to fix the bottom of it. It was still upright. Men were hopping over the side and climbing down a rope ladder. She went down after them simply because she supposed she ought to follow their suit.

As soon as she hit the ground, she felt that the world was spinning around her. She stumbled forward and was about to fall when strong, coarse hands gripped her and held her up. It was Avery Addison. She was able to put his name to his face easily as he was the only crewmember of African descent.

"Are you alright, Miss Bradford?" he asked.

"Just dizzy is all."

"It'll take a while to get used to land again after being at sea for so long."

"Yes, this isn't the first time I've experienced this," Alice said. "Thank you, Mister Addison, I think I'm fine now." Addison left her, glancing back once to be sure she was still was on her feet and that the dizzy spell had, in fact, passed.

The low tide replaced the high. Alice stood back and watched in awe as the *Vengeance Dragon* slowly tipped over with the receding shoreline. Soon it was completely on its side, its bottom exposed. The pirates started scraping barnacles off of the wood, working both fast and thoroughly. Others reinforced weak spots, and others still cleaned larger items that had been removed from the ship altogether, such as the cannons.

Alice moved a bit away from the operation and sat in the shade of the tree line. From here she was able to see everyone at once, which she liked. The natives that had stayed on the beach milled about, checking out the cannons or chatting to the pirates if they knew English.

Captain Boswell kept glancing at the sea, looking for any sign of danger, but especially for any sign of the British navy. Alice could just imagine how hopeless that situation would be. The pirates would be outnumbered and outgunned with no escape. If they tried to fight they would be killed, she knew. But she also knew Captain Boswell would do everything in his power to prevent his being taken.

She suddenly realized that if the navy did attack, she would be free. The sailors would bring her to her mother in England. She would not have to witness any more plundering, any more murder. She would not have to spend another day on the deck of a ship, facing every danger that came with it. She would go home. She would embrace her mother. She would be happy.

But, Alice thought, all of these young men would die, either in the initial battle or later, publicly. Men she had come to know. And Captain Boswell would be taken or killed. His papers would be scattered. His ship would be destroyed. He would never again look out across the ocean as he was so fond of doing.

A rustling from the jungle gained Alice's attention. Some tribal members, including women and children walked out onto the beach. It seemed that they were here to check out the pirates. The children ran ahead and attempted to climb the *Vengeance Dragon* and received a scolding from the adults, prompting a round of laughter from the pirates.

A young girl approached Alice. They were about the same age. Alice tried to be polite, although she was unnerved by the girl's wild appearance and wasn't sure how to proceed when she realized that neither knew the other's language.

Still, the girl plopped down next to Alice and started drawing shapes in the sand with her finger. Before long, both children were lying on their stomachs with a sketch stretched out before them, one half of a primitive village and the other of a neighborhood in England.

After some time, the natives started returning to the jungle, having seen all there was to see. Alice's new acquaintance stood and smiled before running off after her friends. With nothing else to do, Alice scooted backward against a tree and closed her eyes, feeling the warm sun on her face and listening to the soft lapping of the waves. She ended up dozing off for the rest of the six hours.

Alice woke to the sound of the men finishing their work. Their pace eased up from its former steady productivity, and this change in atmosphere was all it took to wake her. The sun had travelled through the sky, creating some shade. Alice sat up and yawned. The bottom of the *Vengeance Dragon* looked sublime and the tide seemed to be once again rising. Captain Boswell was definitely more at ease than he had been before, now that the operation was almost over.

Alice stood up and returned to the vicinity of the crew, stepping deftly over her drawing in the sand so as not to ruin it. The men had begun packing up and the *Vengeance Dragon* was already righting itself as the tide rose.

"You're covered in sand!" Jerome laughed when Alice neared. "It's even in your hair!"

Alice grinned. "My hair looks like yours now. We could be proper siblings."

"We're getting ready to go," Reuben said, hobbling over to the two of them. "Best be getting up onto the ship."

Jerome swept his hand toward the ladder. "Ladies first." Smiling, Alice took hold of a rung.

A young native came running down the beach, shouting, "British! British!"

Alice whirled around and instinctively looked for Captain Boswell. He had been standing off to the side, conversing with Titus, his arms crossed. Now he dropped his arms, his face drained of blood, his eyes wide. The entire area went quiet.

Captain Boswell seized the man by the arm. He hissed, "What did you say?"

"I am sorry," the native panted. "They came before. We said nothing, but they came. They brought guns for us. Now they come again."

"Hurry it up!" Captain Boswell yelled over his shoulder at his men. His voice cracked. The men scurried like mice to get everything back on the ship. Then the captain shook the native's arm. "What are you talking about, man?"

"I am sorry. I am sorry."

Another native now approached. He was older and had been on the beach the moment the *Vengeance Dragon* arrived. His expression was stern.

"He's trying to tell you that the British have come before. They offered us triple of what you always bring in exchange for information about you. We denied you ever came here. But they promised to come again. They have come to us, to our neighbors, to our enemies. Everyone. They are searching for you."

"And they're coming now? Why didn't you tell me any of this?!" The captain was filled with wild panic, panic that he didn't even try to hide.

"It was a good offer."

Captain Boswell took a step back and looked about him. His crew had frozen once again, their mouths agape. His order for them to continue getting ready to leave came out as a near scream.

"You're going to keep us here and collect your reward?" he asked the native.

The native regarded Captain Boswell carefully. His expression was calm and cool. "No."

Captain Boswell felt his breath catch.

"Go quickly," the native continued. "We were wrong to consider their offer. Go before they see you. Do not come here again. It will not be safe." He bowed his head. "I *am* sorry. Now go!"

Captain Boswell turned his back on the native and ran. Water had come up onto the beach and he sloshed through it. Alice pushed herself up the rope ladder and onto the ship. A number of men followed her hurriedly. Titus gathered some of the strongest and had them push on the *Vengeance Dragon*, gritting their teeth and putting their full strength into it, trying to accelerate its backward movement down the beach and into deeper waters.

A British flag appeared over the treetops, displayed prominently from the tip of a frigate's mainmast. Alice gasped at the sight of it. That was her flag. Those were her people on that ship.

Her line of sight was broken by Captain Boswell as he boarded the *Vengeance Dragon* and went straight to the helm. He looked just plain awful, his face pale and a hand on his stomach like he might be sick. The ship shuddered and everyone on board stumbled as it was set free. Titus and the others trudged through almost knee deep water to the ladder. Once they had all boarded or were on their way up, Isaac Owen turned the ship around.

Captain Boswell hunched over the stern-most bulwarks, his elbows resting on the wood. The *Vengeance Dragon* sailed around the island, hugging the shoreline, in the opposite direction from which the British frigate was approaching. Captain Boswell kept his eyes locked on that flag as it was his only indicator of the ship's location.

"Come on, come on," he murmured.

The prow of the frigate appeared.

And then it disappeared as the *Vengeance Dragon* rounded the island, each ship becoming invisible to the other.

Captain Boswell bent his head and closed his eyes briefly, letting out a very long, slow breath. The men clapped each other's backs and some released their tension through laughter.

"Get us far away from here," the captain said to Owen as he departed from the quarter deck. The helmsman nodded. They were the only two people not smiling. Alice made three.

Captain Boswell went to his cabin and was temporarily impeded by his own door. He couldn't get it open for a few seconds because his hand was shaking so badly. Alice saw this display and shook her head. She followed after him.

Inside, the captain had retrieved a bottle of alcohol and a glass and was trying to pour himself a drink. Alice walked in just as he missed the glass and spilled some of the dark liquid onto the desk. Alice hurried to take the bottle from his hands before he could drop it which she was convinced he was about to do.

"You should sit," she told him firmly.

He didn't say anything. He didn't even look at her. Keeping a hand on the desk to steady himself, he moved around to his chair and seemed to flop down just as his legs gave out. Alice sniffed at the alcohol.

"Are you sure you want to drink this?" Alice asked dubiously. The captain glanced up at her and gave her a face like that was a pointless question. Alice relented and sighed, "Alright." She filled the glass about halfway for him.

She held it out to him. When he reached to take it, she put her hand over his and pressed it into the glass, making sure he had a solid grip, not trusting him to hold it on his own. She could feel him trembling. She let go of him and grabbed the bottle to put it away, using it as an excuse to turn away. She felt self-conscious seeing him like this.

The drink cabinet was nearly empty since Captain Boswell had given away almost everything that had been inside it after the storm. Alice gently placed the bottle inside. She heard him put the glass down.

"I'm sorry," he said quietly to her back. She realized he must be feeling much more embarrassed than she was.

"Don't be."

"I can usually hide it. It's just, we've never been this close to… to being caught before."

Alice turned around. The glass was empty already. The captain still had his hand on it. He stared at the desk in front of him.

"But you didn't get caught," Alice said. "There's no point in continuing to think on it. How close of a call it was is irrelevant. This moment belongs to you now. Live it."

Captain Boswell looked at her at last. Some light had returned to his eyes. A small smile touched his lips. "You are quite an extraordinary girl, Alice Bradford. Thank you."

The crew reestablished their routine quickly enough. After making sure Captain Boswell was okay, Alice joined them. She found she enjoyed their company. And it seemed they enjoyed hers. She found herself spending more time on the main deck than in the cabin.

It was a few days later when she was invited to watch a card game by Francis Wesley who wanted to teach her how to play. Alice stood behind him, and he sat in a circle with three men from the gunnery crew, Oliver Griffith, Hugh Clinton, and Adam Paisley. They used a crate as a table, playing cards spread across it.

"All in," Griffith said smugly, pushing his stack of coins into the pot and purposefully putting his cards down. Clinton and Paisley shared a disappointed look.

"Oh, come on," Francis said. "I am not playing with you anymore."

"What?" Griffith asked, feigning exaggerated innocence.

"Let's see your sleeves," Clinton said as a mother might to a misbehaving child. "Come on, out with it."

Griffith turned away. "No."

"You realize you've just implicated yourself, don't you?"

Alice had to cover mouth with her hands to stifle the laughter that was threatening to escape her as Paisley started grappling with Griffith, trying to roll up his sleeves. The struggling itself was all it took to loosen up the cards that Griffith was indeed hiding and they slipped to the deck.

"And that's a wrap," Clinton said, collecting his coins, even those which he had lost since the start of the game. The others did the same.

"Too bad we don't have someone to trade our money with, ever since the incident with Reed," Griffith muttered.

Titus overheard that statement. He shot Griffith a glare. Before anything could be said, however, a ship emerged from shallow waters. It dropped anchor at the sight of the *Vengeance Dragon* and raised a white flag.

"Someone get the captain," Titus said. "No one take your eyes off that ship."

CHAPTER TWENTY-ONE

~ 1716, Summer ~

I SAW JANE OFTEN, or at least as often as the crew and I returned to port. We didn't spend much time together, but to me it was valuable time. We were friends and nothing more. I think part of me longed to be closer to her. As I got to know her, I no longer fell under that gawking spell that used to cause me to stare whenever I saw her. Jane was beautiful, and I always thought so, but as our friendship grew I came to appreciate her kindness more than anything.

The knowledge that she would soon be married hung heavy on me. It was like a cloud that followed us everywhere. Had this not have been the case, would we have pursued a more intimate relationship? I don't know how she felt about it, and though I tried not to admit it to myself, it was what I wished.

Anytime I was not on that navy ship, Jane put my mind at ease. Yet whenever I sailed on it, I felt that I was deteriorating under a cruel and hate-filled power. The officers and the other sailors looked down on me. They always had. But it was finally having an effect on my mentality. The wall that I had built up when I was first thrown into the navy, the wall to protect myself from straying from my desire to remain dutiful and obedient, was breaking down. The more it broke, the more it was replaced by a wall meant to protect me from harm.

I distrusted everyone. I grew to hate them all. It wasn't just that they looked down on me. It was that they absolutely believed they were better than me, as if I was some sort of lesser human being. I think I always knew it, but for the first time I openly acknowledged it. I thought that this line of thinking had started when I was flogged. Now I know it had started the day I was sold.

How could they think me no better than a slave? It made my blood boil in anger. I did my work and I did it efficiently without complaint, no matter how terribly I was treated. Yet they still saw me as nothing more than a commodity to be exploited. They had paid for me. Did that not amount to some sort of worth? Was I truly not valuable to them?

To the man who sold me: Did you not even see some value in me? Was a sack of money all it took to turn you from a kindly fisherman, to warn me to stay away from the impressment gang, into a greedy, betraying, hypocrite?

To the sailor who strikes me: Do you really think I am so far below you, even though we are both deckhands from a poor family? And even if I was below you, how does that give you the right to treat me like this?

To Lieutenant Benjamin Madison: Who do you think you are? Rank and authoritative power are necessary for order, yet you abuse both. What have I done that has caused you to hate me?

To Commodore George Madison: How do you have no compassion, no understanding? You have more power than anyone in the navy. You are in charge of all of us. You are like a king. And I hate you for it.

There came a point when I could take it no longer. I needed to leave. I felt I was slowly dying from poison, being on that ship. I knew the dangers of desertion, but it was an absolutely necessary risk I needed to take. I knew I could tell no one of my plan, not even Richard, for my safety and for his.

Once I had resolved myself of this need, I endured another week, knowing that we would soon lay anchor with several other ships at a port among the Caribbean Islands. During that week, I prepared myself, stealing a few items here and there so that no one would know they were gone. By the time I was ready, I had filled a sack with some food, supplies, and clothing. I wasn't thinking much beyond my escape, and so I didn't have a plan for what to do once I reached shore. At the moment, all I cared about was getting to shore at all.

I decided to wait for the early morning before disembarking. I would leave just before the sun rose, giving me at least a little darkness. The final night watch shift would be ending, which meant the men would be less vigilant than if I went earlier when it was darker out. This decision was a gamble, but I thought at the time that I was making the right choice.

I hardly slept that night as I waited for my moment. Below decks it was difficult to tell the time, so I was forced to estimate. When I thought the time was right, I got up and walked silently to the ladder. There was really no reason to be so cautious. Men came and went all night. But I didn't want to risk anyone asking me questions, and I thought it would be safest to avoid people as much as possible.

When I reached the deck, I was dismayed to find that I was just a bit later than I hoped. The sun hadn't risen yet, but there was a haze of muted light in the air suggesting that it was about to. I hesitated, wondering if I should wait for the next day, but ultimately decided to go through with my plan. I had been anxious to get going from the start and I feared delay.

I slung the sack over my shoulder, hanging onto it with one hand, and then slowly walked to the nearest bulwark. I tried my hardest not to attract attention. There were several men up and about, as well as some men on the commodore's ship next to mine. The shore was within sight, about fifty meters away, and that's all I was focused on.

I dropped the sack by my feet. I placed my hands on the bulwarks and leaned over the edge, looking down. The water gently lapped at the wood of the ship some feet below. I would have to carefully climb down so that when I entered the water there would be no splash.

"Boswell!"

I jumped at the sound of my name and whirled around in a moment of panic. A senior sailor stood there, his arms crossed as he looked at me questioningly.

"What are you doing?" He seemed genuinely curious, so I decided to play the fool and shrugged, figuring it would be the most convincing act since they all thought me incompetent anyway. Unfortunately, the sailor walked closer to me, my act an apparent invitation for him to come and pry.

"I wasn't doing anything," I said quickly.

He looked at me carefully. Another sailor stopped what he was doing to look on. I decided in that instant to just walk away, to wait for tomorrow to make my escape. I bent down and picked up my sack. That was a mistake.

"What is that?" the first sailor asked. "What's in there?"

The second sailor had come closer and they both now stood in my way. I made to push past them and be on my way but neither moved. My panic grew. I pushed harder and so did they. They also rose their voices. I should have just stopped but I was feeling trapped, as if they already knew what I was planning.

Two more men came. If it had been anyone else, they would've let the incident go. But it was me, and after the day of my whipping I had become renowned for being disobedient, even though that had been my only offence.

Someone grabbed the sack from me and we each pulled on it for a few seconds before he finally won it from me, dumping out the contents. Since I knew it wasn't worth the effort to keep trying to get passed them, I made a desperate lunge for the bulwarks, hoping to jump overboard. Hands grabbed me and pulled me back. Someone shouted, "Deserter!" There was no question about it. Between the sack of necessities and my attempt to jump just now, it was clear to them that I had been trying to desert.

My next mistake was to fight against the hands that held me. I felt trapped and claustrophobic. My need to get away had never been stronger. Amid my wrestling, I saw Lieutenant Madison emerge from his quarters with another officer, responding to the commotion that I had caused. One of the sailors ran to them and I saw him speak quickly, a finger pointed at me. They marched briskly over, Lieutenant Madison's eyes locked on me.

"Hold him!" the lieutenant barked. The hands clenched around my arms tightened. "Fetch the captain and the cat o' nine."

My heart stopped at his words, I'm sure. He stared at me with malice like I had never seen from him. I suddenly had no hatred for him. No, all I had was fear.

CHAPTER TWENTY-TWO

C APTAIN BOSWELL HAD BEEN IN HIS CABIN. Now he stood next to Owen at the helm's wheel and instructed the man to get in close enough to determine who was on board the stranger ship.

"It's a ship fit for pirates," Titus pointed out.

"I thought the same," Captain Boswell said.

The *Vengeance Dragon* approached and Owen spun the helm's wheel, turning the ship a little to keep her distance. The men on the stranger ship wore no kind of uniform. The ship itself, despite its small size and ability to sail through shallow water, was outfitted with cannons. One man stood on the bulwarks, waving his arms, flagging down the *Vengeance Dragon*.

"Unless they've disguised themselves, they're definitely pirates," Titus said.

Captain Boswell nodded. "I agree. But if it took us this long to figure that out, how did they know that they could trust us as soon as they saw us?"

"Perhaps they're desperate for aid. They saw the *Vengeance Dragon*, saw her size, and decided to risk assuming that we're fellow pirates."

Captain Boswell wasn't too sure. All the same, he said to Owen, "Bring us in a little closer, close enough to talk to them. We'll see what they want, help where we can, and leave as quickly as possible. We'll just have to hope that they don't describe us to anyone who knows who we are."

Then he leaned over the railing to look across the main deck, seeking out Alice. He didn't need to raise his voice much to be heard for the crew had become rather silent. "Alice." She turned to look at him. "I need you to stay in the cabin, please. They'll question your presence if they see you. It could complicate matters." Alice nodded, fully understanding, and obeyed.

The *Vengeance Dragon* pulled up alongside the pirate ship. Quite a few meters still separated them. The pirate captain now stood middeck of his ship, waiting for them. He wore a large, tricorn hat. Captain Boswell walked to the middle of his own ship and met him.

"Thank you for stopping," the pirate captain called. "Captain Gandy is my name. We have sick men on board. Do you have a medicine chest that we may use?"

"I'm afraid all we have is a medical bag, and most of its contents have been used already. It won't be much use to you," Captain Boswell answered back.

"I'll take anything I can get. Do you mind bringing it over? I'll give you any supplies you might need in exchange."

Captain Boswell swore inwardly. He had hoped his answer, although true, would be unsatisfactory to Captain Gandy, allowing him to be on his way. "Please excuse me for being wary, but I would prefer if one of your men came and retrieved it."

Captain Gandy was silent for a heartbeat. "Of course, of course! In fact, I'll come over with them, as a token of trust."

Captain Boswell didn't like that idea any more than the first. It also struck him how he had deliberately requested that one man come, while Captain Gandy had used the word *them*. Still, there was no way to back out without causing suspicion and so he consented. He ordered the crew to stand by and be prepared for absolutely anything to happen. But most importantly, he told them to relax and act natural.

As the two ships drew in to each other, Captain Boswell noticed with apprehension that Captain Gandy's crew was over double the size of his own. He thought it odd that such a small ship would need so many men, and now that he thought about it they did seem a bit crowded. He also saw that aside from the normal number of cannon ports, the ship also had quite a few cannons mounted on its prow and stern.

The ships were tied together and a gangplank connected them. Captain Gandy walked across it, flanked by five other men. Captain Boswell stood erect, trying to keep his gaze steady, waiting to receive them. Titus stood by him with the medical bag and his presence gave him confidence.

"Welcome aboard," Captain Boswell said, shaking the other captain's hand. Then he stepped aside for Titus who handed over the medical bag. Captain Gandy took it and passed it back to one of his men. None of them turned to leave.

"Is there anything else we can do for you?" Captain Boswell asked tentatively.

Captain Gandy kept his expression neutral. "What was your name, sir?"

There was only a brief hesitation. "Captain Wilson." It was the name he had used with Reed, and it was all he could think of.

"Ah, there was a Captain Wilson that used to frequent a trader by the name of Mister Reed. I visited Reed regularly myself. Until he turned up dead in his own shop, that is." Captain Gandy stared hard at Captain Boswell, and the latter did his best to betray nothing.

"Reed's death was quite a shock," was all he said.

Captain Gandy squinted. "Your crew is small."

Had that been meant as a threat? "Yes... I've lost men over the years."

"And you haven't signed any more on to replace them?"

Captain Boswell became uncomfortable. "No." He looked past Captain Gandy at the men that the other pirate had brought over. Their swords caught his eye for the first time. "Are those military issue swords?"

Captain Gandy glanced back at them. "Why, yes. Many of my men are deserters from the navy."

Captain Boswell took a half step back. He tried to make the movement look natural, as if he had just been shifting his weight. Warily, he swept his eyes from one end of Captain Gandy's ship to the other. The other man's crew was lined up along the bulwarks, watching the exchange. Half of them were wearing these military swords.

Captain Boswell chose his words carefully. "With all due respect, sir, I think it time we parted ways."

Several seconds passed. Captain Boswell resisted the urge to look at Titus. At last, Captain Gandy nodded and slowly turned to the left. His hand abruptly went to his sword and he turned back while drawing the weapon, swinging in an arch toward Captain Boswell. Captain Boswell deftly drew his rapier and halted the sudden attack with a clash. Both crews grabbed their weapons, swords and pistols alike, waiting for the order to attack.

"I thought it was you, Stephen Boswell, but I had to be sure. The need for aid was a ruse," Captain Gandy said. "Now surrender and your crew will be spared."

"I can't do that," Captain Boswell said through gritted teeth.

Captain Gandy was eerily calm as he spoke. "Each of your men has a gun aimed at them by two of my men. Even if one misses, the other surely will not. Even if both miss, even if your men manage to take out some of mine, then what? They will still have to face the rest."

"We will fight and we may die, but we will not become prisoners of the British." The two men disengaged their swords, the sound of rasping metal filling the air.

"Bold words coming from a man who fears death." Captain Gandy smiled and his men sniggered. "Let's make it interesting, shall we? No point in risking my men's lives over your mulishness. I propose a duel. Captain to captain. It'd be most entertaining. What say you?"

"What are your terms?" Captain Boswell asked, daring to feel a bit of hope.

"If I win, then you and your crew surrenders to me. If you win, then I let you and your crew sail away. It won't be to the death of course. The bounty will be much higher if you're alive. The duel will take place on my ship. After all, I know it better than yours. As for weapons, I've heard you're an excellent shot, and so pistols are out of the question, and it's well known that the rapier is your preferred sword. Therefore, I choose cutlasses."

Captain Boswell narrowed his eyes. "Those terms are absurd and you know it. As the challenged party-"

"You are not the challenged party, you are the party that is about to be slaughtered if you do not accept," Captain Gandy interrupted. "I am giving you a chance to save your men. If you win, you get to sail away, as I've said. Yes, I will come after you. Yes, I will have support from the British navy. No, you won't be able to escape. But your men will be able to."

"Who are you?"

Captain Gandy's smile returned. "Privateer, under commission by King George. One of the best. Half of these men have been loaned to me by the navy. They're desperate to find you, the navy. They gave me all the information they could to help them. Before the commission I was a pirate like you. I know what your men must mean to you."

"And how did you find me?"

"It was chance, mostly. Tracked you this far. If it wasn't for a drawing of England in the sand and an easily intimidated young native, we would've lost you. We had to guess which direction you'd go next. As you can see we guessed right. Just had to make sure it was really you and that we hadn't flagged down a random ship that happened to be in the area. It wasn't difficult to identify you. Black hair, dark eyes. They told me your crew might be small. You never leave witnesses alive and probably never recruit.

Above all, you have trust issues. You, sir, fit the description perfectly. But now back to what really matters. Do you accept my terms or shall I order my men to attack?"

Captain Boswell looked to Titus. The two friends didn't need to speak words to communicate. Next he gazed across his men, meeting each of their eyes, making sure they knew what was expected of them. Their expressions were stern. They knew what to do. They were ready.

"I accept your terms," Captain Boswell said.

CHAPTER TWENTY-THREE

~ 1716, Summer ~

HANDS GRASPED MY ARMS and men surrounded me. Lieutenant Madison stood with another officer, waiting for the dreaded whip to be brought to him so that he could punish me for my attempted desertion.

"No, no, no, no," I stammered. I saw someone bring rope. "No!" I thrashed as if I had been drowning, kicking and pulling like my life depended on it, which I felt it did. I managed to knock over one man, but all that gained me was two more jumping in to help. I could not endure another whipping, I just couldn't.

Then I spotted Richard. He stood off to the side, but close by, watching everything warily. I made eye contact and silently pleaded to him for help. I know to have done so was selfish. He was my friend, and to put pressure on him to risk his own safety was low of me. But I was desperate and frantic. Once I had made my plea, I saw no hesitation in him. His eyes narrowed in resolved determination and I instantly knew that he would do everything in his power to help me.

He walked over, purpose in his stride, and took a handful of the nearest man's shirt collar. Surprised, the man turned and was met with a fist to the face. Richard then pulled on the shoulder of someone who was restraining me and hit him in a similar way. Now with one arm free I was able to scramble away from the hold on my other.

The group of men had by now realized that Richard was a threat and turned some of their focus to him. I knew that Richard was trying to give me an escape route and I tried to take it but I was being jostled around and couldn't get my bearings straight. I was knocked to the wood beneath me.

I saw Richard square up against the men, his fists raised. I also saw Lieutenant Madison approach the scuffle with a hand touching the foil sheathed at his side.

As I struggled to stand, I saw the boots of the other officer just in front of me. Instead of finding my feet, I lurched forward into him, bringing us both down. I put a knee to his chest and pressed down hard while I quickly fumbled for the hilt of his sword. When I found it, I drew the foil and stood up, turning around to face the others, placing a kick in the officer's face midway for good measure.

I held the foil out before me, grasping it with both hands, my legs spread apart, trying to mime how I had seen the officers stand before when I watched them fence. The scuffle paused, no one sure of how to react to the new threat that I posed, even if pathetic. That is, until the lieutenant put his hand up and motioned for the men to back away and make room.

He didn't say a word. He took a few steps forward. He looked at me. I could read no expression on his face. Then he pulled his foil from its scabbard and pointed it at me.

My mouth was dry and I couldn't hold the sword steady. My arm shook slightly and I was breathing hard. Lieutenant Madison looked confident and comfortable. We stood like this for an eternity. I know now that he was waiting for me to make the first move and that he would have waited as long as it took.

I lunged, aiming for his face. The point of the sword shot closer to his left shoulder. The outcome wouldn't have changed had I been able to aim more skillfully. He hardly seemed to move. His foil was like a flash, tapping my attack aside with ease and sliding down the length of my sword and circumventing the handguard to slice the back of my wrist.

I dropped the sword with a gasp. The lieutenant stepped up to me, seized me by the shirt, and brought the hilt of his sword down on my cheek. I fell, my face stinging with pain.

"You're nothing but dirt," he spat at me. "You will be punished severely, I can promise you that."

I used my arms to pull myself forward, away from him. I knew I wouldn't be able to make it anywhere, but still my desire to escape propelled me. That's when I saw a pistol sitting atop a barrel, just an arm's length away. Jenkin's pistol, I knew. He was always leaving it around.

I heard the lieutenant's boots as he paced slowly by me, taunting me. All I focused on was that gun. Slowly, I dragged myself toward it. I had reached the barrel when I heard the lieutenant's taunts falter. As I pulled myself up I turned to look at him and saw that his eyes had grown wide. He had seen the gun.

I snatched it and aimed. His face went pale. There were no thoughts in my head. I was empty. I don't remember the moment exactly. I don't remember deciding to shoot, or even registering that there was a decision to be made. I just remember knowing that I was going to do it, when movement on the ship next to ours caught my attention.

At first I just turned my head. I saw the commodore standing there and he was yelling something. Then my arm turned until the gun was pointing at him. And then I pulled the trigger.

The gun bucked in my hand as smoke poured from it, the sound of the shot ringing out. I saw the commodore lurch, blood splattering like juice from an exploding fruit. His arms went out as he fell backwards.

Lieutenant Madison shouted. I ran to the edge of the ship and dove overboard, the gun in my hand leading my jump. I landed in the water between the two ships and let my momentum carry me downward and, hopefully, out of sight of the men above. Then I swam as hard as I could toward the shore.

CHAPTER TWENTY-FOUR

THE OPPONENTS FACED EACH OTHER. Captain Boswell held Titus' cutlass. He stood on the deck of Captain Gandy's ship surrounded by both crews. They formed a large oval, the space inside clear except for the mainmast. Captain Boswell took a moment to look for his men. They were dispersed throughout the crowd. He glanced at the cabin of the *Vengeance Dragon*. He couldn't see Alice, but he knew she was watching somehow.

Lastly, Captain Boswell looked at Titus. His friend stood just behind him and gave him a nod.

Captain Gandy extended his arms, one hand holding onto his sword, and his crew cheered. Then he and Captain Boswell approached each other. The crowd hushed expectantly. Each captain stared at the other in ready stances. There was no signal for the duel to begin.

Captain Gandy attacked first. He sprang forward, leading with his sword, and Captain Boswell parried, forced to retreat a few steps. His last step was to the side and as his sword met Captain Gandy's, he sent the other man stumbling forward. Captain Boswell used the moment to catch his breath and remind himself to breathe. He caught Titus' eye briefly. His first mate was tense.

Captain Gandy turned around after regaining his footing. He did not look pleased. He pressed forward, on the offensive again, striking right, left, right, left, in quick succession. Captain Boswell blocked each blow, not thinking so much as feeling where each strike was going to land. On his last strike, Captain Gandy shifted his weight, giving him some leverage in forcing Captain Boswell's sword down as he blocked. The privateer then stepped in and knocked his shoulder into Captain Boswell's chest.

The force had not been strong, yet Captain Boswell was momentarily stunned by the sudden physical contact. Captain Gandy slid his sword away from Captain Boswell's and slashed upward at his arm in one motion. Captain Boswell pivoted away, avoiding the attack, yet failed to bring his sword back up quickly. Now at the top of his sweep, Captain Gandy reversed direction and abruptly brought his sword down diagonally to the right, slicing across Captain Boswell's upper arm.

Captain Boswell let out a hiss of pain at the sudden sting but that was all. He backed away from Captain Gandy and rounded the deck so he was standing back where he had when the duel began, hoping to gain even a few seconds to rest. The bout had lasted but seconds. He was used to the long reach of a rapier and felt ill at ease to be in such close quarters with Captain Gandy. The cutlass' ability to slice had also caught him off guard. Sure, a rapier's blade edge could do some damage, but it was primarily a thrusting sword and all Captain Boswell knew how to use effectively.

Captain Boswell glanced at Titus. His first mate gave a nod. They both knew who was going to win this fight, and they were prepared.

Having tested Captain Boswell's skill, Captain Gandy now pressed his advantage by coming in close once again. He came fast. His feet moved like a dancer's and his sword flashed like a snake. Their weapons locked, their faces inches from each other. Captain Gandy was stronger and quickly gained the upper hand. The privateer hooked a leg behind Captain Boswell. Hoping to speed up the inevitable outcome without sustaining any more injuries, Captain Boswell loosened up and let his opponent neatly push him down onto his back.

Captain Boswell had tried to take the move with ease, allowing Captain Gandy to take him down without resistance, yet he still landed hard and felt his breath escape him. Captain Gandy stepped on the pirate captain's forearm, keeping it still and its sword at bay. He pointed his own sword's point at Captain Boswell's face and smiled.

He opened his mouth to speak, but someone beat him to it.

"Stop!"

Every privateer turned to stare at the young girl that had appeared in the doorway of the *Vengeance Dragon*'s cabin. A low murmuring spread across the deck as the privateers voiced their surprise. Captain Gandy opened and closed his mouth a few times.

Captain Boswell looked to Titus. Titus had already drawn his pistol and the pirates had done the same. They gave no warning. They each fired point blank at a privateer simultaneously, then either drew a second pistol, took the pistol of the fallen man they had just killed, or drew swords and repeated. In just a few seconds Captain Gandy's crew had been reduced by over two-thirds.

The remaining privateers fumbled for their weapons, but their reaction time was too slow. Not only had they been unprepared, but Alice's presence had left them fixated. Those that had managed to react found themselves outnumbered by three to one or more. Others were cut down as they reacted and never really had an opportunity to defend themselves. In just a few seconds more, the entire crew had been dispatched. They never stood a chance.

During this time, Captain Boswell swept his legs under Captain Gandy, knocking him heavily to the deck. Captain Boswell regained his feet and kicked his opponent's sword out of reach. He brought his own sword up with two hands, ready to bring it down and end the privateer's life.

Captain Gandy was smiling. Smiling at himself, it seemed, at having not seen this ambush coming.

"No witnesses," he said knowingly, still smiling. "Do what you have to do. Don't let those sons of bitches catch you."

Captain Boswell nodded meaningfully. He brought the sword down.

He looked across the two ships at Alice. She had both hands over her mouth, her eyes wide with horror at having witnessed that much killing in such a short amount of time. He looked away from her and closed his eyes, forcing himself to breathe. Someone touched his shoulder. It was Titus.

"We can take care of this. Go relax." Titus' faced spread into a grin. "You had me real nervous, you know that?"

Captain Boswell handed the sword to his friend. "Yeah, how do you think I felt?" He lowered his voice. "How bad was I?"

"Oh, no, not bad at all, no." Titus shook his head. "Okay, no, yes, you were terrible. Did you let him take you at the end?"

Captain Boswell shrugged. "I didn't want him to hurt me."

"That sentence is… very interesting." Titus burst into laughter, although half of it was more out of relief than it was humor. Captain Boswell allowed himself a small smile before leaving.

He crossed the gangplank and felt more at ease to be on his own ship again. He came to a stop in front of Alice. She met his eyes although she was clearly unnerved.

"Did I… did I cause that?" she asked, her voice shaking.

Captain Boswell stepped forward, concerned. "No. No, Alice. We had planned for that to happen. You didn't cause it. Are you okay?"

She put a hand on her forehead. "I'm fine, I think. I thought he was going to kill you. I just, I had to stop him."

"It wasn't to the death, Alice."

Alice slid her hand down to her cheek. "Oh! Oh my. I feel silly now."

"Don't. Let's go inside."

There was not enough room on the *Vengeance Dragon* to hold all of the cargo from the privateer ship. Most of the cargo consisted of weapons, gunpowder, and ammunition. The pirates eagerly filled up their stores, and Hugh Clinton and his gunners were most excited to finally have a full row of cannonballs lined up next to the cannons. In fact, he and Adam Paisley shared a drunken embrace at which the rest of the crew laughed. All sorts of tools were brought over as well as materials such as rope, wood, and metal, and even a fully stocked medicine chest. It seemed that most of these items had come from the British, either gifted or loaned. Once the *Vengeance Dragon*'s hold became full, the pirates resorted to stacking boxes and barrels on the main deck. When Titus handed Captain Boswell the long list of inventory, the latter man was speechless.

Reuben prepared nothing short of a feast that evening. As the sun set, a celebration broke out on the ship. There were plenty of drinks to go round. Some of the men started a card game, although they wouldn't allow Oliver Griffith to join in. Jerome struck up a tune and others sat around, singing along and clapping. And some became inebriated.

The mood aboard the *Vengeance Dragon* was as light as Alice had ever seen it. She could forget for a moment all she had seen and experienced. She could forget who these people were and what they had done. She could even sit by Captain Boswell, expressing her concern over his injured arm, asking about the duel and swordsmanship in general, just two acquaintances having a conversation.

Nevertheless, no one knew it then that this peace was not to last. The British were waiting. Their prized privateer had failed. But the navy had yet to try.

CHAPTER TWENTY-FIVE

~ 1716, Summer ~

I SWAM UNDERWATER UNTIL MY LUNGS burned for air. My muscles started to go numb and I could no longer use my full strength to keep propelling myself forward. My vision had also started to grow spotty and I knew that I needed to risk surfacing.

When I looked up I could see sunlight. I aimed for it, fighting through the water. My head emerged and I gulped down breaths of air. Behind me, rowboats were being dropped into the water from the ships and armed men were piling in. The sight spurred me on and I resumed my swim.

The splashing of paddles let me know how far back my pursuers were. Just as they started to gain on me, my feet felt solid ground. I stood, grateful to give my arms a rest, and struggled to wade the rest of the way.

"Fire at will!" I heard Lieutenant Madison order, and I immediately dropped to my stomach, bullets whizzing by me. As the men reloaded, I made it to the edge of the water and stumbled with the sudden lack of resistance to my legs, sand clinging to my clothes and hands.

I broke into a run. Buildings and structures stood a ways to my right, expanding deeper into the island. I ran parallel to them, aiming for the brush beyond the shore.

The navy sailors fired their weapons again. I hunched my shoulders and tried to keep my head low. Sand flew at me from bullets hurling into the ground, just missing my legs. Lieutenant Madison screamed orders like a madman.

The rowboats made it onto the beach and the men hopped out of them into shallow water. The brush was just ahead of me. I clenched my teeth pumped my arms, my legs stretching forward.

Gunshots ripped through the air a third time. I leaped over some low bushes and let myself drop as I landed, rolling onto my shoulder. The leaves whistled as the bullets flew through them.

Tall, tropical trees surrounded me. There was green all around. I ran past it all, my feet pounding the ground.

I remember thinking to myself that I would run until I died, that I would let myself die of exhaustion before allowing those men to take my life themselves.

Giant leaves slapped my face as I went past, and branches grabbed at my legs. The swim had already sapped me of most of my strength, and the sudden threat of the men on the beach had only given me a temporary rush of adrenaline. Now even that was failing.

The burn in my lungs returned, although this time there was plenty of air available around me. My legs also burned, my muscles screaming painfully for respite. Yet I dared not stop, not even for a second.

At last I could not keep going. I collapsed on the spot, my legs refusing to respond. I couldn't even lift my arms to break my fall. I landed with my face in the dirt, and I could not lift my head. It wasn't until then that I became consciously aware of the gun still in my hand, and even then my fingers remained tightly wrapped around the grip.

My chest heaved violently and I gasped audibly. I thought for sure that the navy men would bear down on me at any minute, emerging from the brush with their weapons drawn and pointed at me.

"Stephen!"

My heart sank when I heard my name. With apprehension, I looked for the voice, only to be flooded with relief as I saw Richard running toward me. When he got close, he stiffened one leg, sliding to a stop and falling beside me. He grabbed me by the shoulders and rolled me over onto my back.

"How did you get here?" I mumbled, panting.

"Soon as you pulled that gun, no one paid any attention to me," he said. "Until you fired I didn't know what you were gonna do, but once you did, I knew you'd jump and swim for shore. So I ran to the part of the ship closest to shore before jumping in myself and got here before you."

"How did you find me? How did you know I'd come this way?"

Richard had by now pulled me up into a sitting position. "All we've been through, Stephen. I know you well. I know you came this way to avoid people, but I think heading to where it's populated will help us lose the navy."

As if on cue, we heard the sounds of men running through the brush, trampling the undergrowth and pounding across the dirt. Only the trees and tall weeds kept us hidden from them, but they wouldn't for long.

Richard stood and grabbed each of my forearms. As he pulled me up, I tried to help by pushing with my legs, but I didn't even have the strength to do that. All the effort came from him, and once I had regained my feet, he continued to hold me up because I threatened to fall over.

We ran awkwardly toward the town, one of my arms around Richard's shoulder. It didn't take long for me to be able to move on my own again. Richard could have gone a lot faster for a much longer time, but he remained at my pace, and I think his presence even helped me to exceed my own limits.

Our speed was constant with that of the navy, and so we remained just out of eyeshot. We broke the tree line and hurried around the corner of the first building that we came to. Just as we rounded it, we heard shouts behind us and knew that we had been seen.

"Come on!" Richard urged. We zigzagged around town, pressing further and further into population. The navy men rarely saw us, only as we turned corners, and when they did they couldn't fire their guns without risking shooting a bystander. We were always one step ahead of them.

But then they split up, with groups of men taking different routes, hoping to cut us off. I was also starting to slow down, my fatigue returning as I reached my physical limit.

We became trapped against the front of a building. A group was still on our tail and another was bearing down on us from ahead, this one led by Lieutenant Madison himself.

I took a deep breath, suddenly realizing the severity of the crime I had just committed. The commodore was the highest ranking man in the navy and I had killed him in front of sailors, in front of officers, in front of the lieutenant, his nephew. And then I thought of Jane. I had just killed her father.

CHAPTER TWENTY-SIX

A FEW DAYS FOLLOWING THE CELEBRATION, the British struck. Their privateer captain had not made contact with them on the agreed upon date. They sailed to the area where Captain Gandy had been lying in wait for the *Vengeance Dragon* and found no sign of him, his crew, or his ship. So they fanned out and searched, knowing that the *Vengeance Dragon* would be nearby. Four ships searched. Four battle-ready, fully stocked, naval warships.

The pirates had created a false sense of safety for themselves. Even Captain Boswell had allowed himself to relax. Alice found it easy to talk to him. She felt a difference in herself, too. She talked more, smiled more, and spent less time in the cabin and more in the company of the men.

The signal light caught everyone off guard. It was like a gold firework, shot straight upward into the sky for all to see for miles. It was the only way the pirates had known a ship was there. And they had been seen first.

The pirates jumped to their posts, scrambling to get the *Vengeance Dragon* moving. Captain Boswell, Titus, and every other man who had people under his command shouted, "Go! Go! Go!"

Isaac Owen had been chatting with Charles Mather, the boatswain, on the quarterdeck and now he snapped himself to the helm's wheel.

"Get us out of here!" Captain Boswell shouted at him. "Any direction, I don't care, just get us away!" Owen turned the ship away, putting the enemy beyond her stern.

Two more ships came to the first's call. They were far away, and spread out. Captain Boswell tried to focus on the first, to tell himself not to worry about the other two because of their distance. Still, the three worried him, and they reminded him of the Spanish attack that had claimed the lives of Miles and Doyle.

"They're British," Titus said, slightly awed.

"Yes, I know that," Captain Boswell snapped. He grabbed onto the hilt of his sword with his left hand, clenching and unclenching his hand around it nervously.

Then one of his men called out a warning from the prow. A fourth ship was racing directly toward the *Vengeance Dragon*. It was slightly larger than the other three, and attached to its prow, level with the surface of the water, was what looked like a large wooden beak, its tip ending in a sharp point.

"They're going to ram us," Captain Boswell said, the realization dawning. "We need more speed. Throw the cargo over! Everything we don't need!"

The men readily complied. Alice stood helplessly in the middle of the main deck, the pirates moving about, tossing boxes, crates, and barrels over the side of the ship as if it were trash, the same cargo that had given cause for celebration just days earlier.

The decrease in weight gave the *Vengeance Dragon* just enough of an edge. The large British ship bore down at an angle, aiming for the center of the hull. The *Vengeance Dragon* seemed to spurt passed, just missing the deadly ram, and Owen turned the ship slightly away.

The two vessels slipped by each other. The navy warship towered over the *Vengeance Dragon*. Captain Boswell stared upward. He looked to the helm. He saw the man in command. He saw the arrogance that the man displayed: chin up, hands clasped calmly behind his back, wide hat on his head, handsome coat over his shoulders, elegant rapier at his side. The men caught each other's eyes.

Titus swore. "Benjamin Madison."

"Benjamin Madison?" Alice repeated, recognition in her voice. She called to the quarter deck, "Did you say Benjamin Madison?"

Titus heard her and quizzically narrowed his eyes. Captain Boswell did not hear her as he was fixated on his enemy. Why was he in command of his own ship? Benjamin Madison seemed to read Captain Boswell's thoughts. He smiled contemptuously and gave a command.

"Fire portside cannons."

The navy ship was in no position to be able to fire its cannons and hit the *Vengeance Dragon*. Owen had made sure of it. The sailors obeyed the command anyway, letting loose a volley from more than one gun deck. Cannonballs tore at the sea, rocking the *Vengeance Dragon* and sending water onto her deck. The pirates covered their ears, deafened by the thunder-like sound. It was a display of power, Captain Boswell knew. A display of vanity.

The *Vengeance Dragon* fled. The four navy ships regrouped and pursued, but they quickly lost sight of the little pirate vessel. They would need to decide their next move. Captain Boswell had the men create as much distance as possible. The stakes were high, yet he was oddly calm, and that scared Alice. Right now, she was reminded of how he had been when they first met: cold and calculating.

CHAPTER TWENTY-SEVEN

~ 1716, Summer ~

TITUS AND I STOOD with our backs to the building, trapped in front of it. Behind us, the door opened and a man stepped out. He looked old to me, his face weathered and wearing a thick, gray beard. He was grizzled and bent forward slightly. He took in the sight of Richard and me standing there, out of breath, and the uniformed men coming at us.

"Get inside." His voice was gruff, even, and emotionless. Richard and I didn't move but only looked at each other. The old man took us each by the base of the back of neck with surprising strength and said, "I'll take care of this, now *get inside*." He sent us through the doorway like two kittens being handled by the scruff of the neck.

We stumbled into the main room. There were no windows that I could see. Light was provided by candles dispersed throughout. There was a bar along the opposite wall and rickety tables filled the area. Yet the first thing that I noticed was all of the men who were staring at Richard and me.

Most of the men had hardened faces and were armed with pistols and cutlasses. There seemed to be a wide range of wealth between them, some wearing large coats and hats while others had not even shoes. There was also an even mix of Europeans, Africans, and native islanders. I was struck by their integration. White men and black men were sitting next to each other at the bar and playing cards and having drinks together at tables. And now they each looked at us with similar mild curiosity.

"The old man sent you in?" the bartender queried, making his voice project across the room. Richard didn't say anything but instead looked at me, clearly dazed.

As shaken as I was, I managed to find my voice. "Yes, sir."

For some reason my reply made the bartender smile. The rest of the men went back to what they were doing and ignored us, light chatter replacing the silence that we had caused.

"Well, whatever trouble you lads are in, the old man'll take care of it," the bartender said.

Richard whispered to me, "What is this?"

I allowed my eyes to wander the room and they were once again drawn to the friendliness between skin colors. The weapons also stuck out to me again, especially the cutlasses. I also saw that the hands of these men were tough and calloused, like sailor hands. The way they all just minded their own business, black and white, rich and poor….

I leaned in to Richard and said almost inaudibly, "I think these men might be pirates."

There were suddenly voices on the other side of the door and Richard and I whirled to face it, expecting it to be flung open or broken down to admit a hoard of navy men.

Instead I heard the old man bark, "Hold it right there!" His words burred with a northern accent.

"You will stand aside." The demand unmistakably came from Lieutenant Madison.

"I will do no such thing."

"There is a criminal in there. We have no fight with you, but if you do not stand aside then we will use force."

"There are two dozen men in there who would love to try their hand at killing some navy bastards, even if it means risking their lives," the old man growled deeply. "We got wind that your ships were on the way over here and we prepared for a fight just in case. What're you prepared for? To start that fight now? Or to catch one criminal?"

There was silence for a moment and then the lieutenant said, "I'm warning you now-"

"And I'm warning *you* now," the old man interrupted. I held my breath, not daring to hope that the old man had done it, had saved us.

There was hushed talking that I couldn't discern, and then I heard Lieutenant Madison order half of the men to guard the entrances to the tavern we were in and the rest to return to the ship. Then the door opened and the old man entered, alone.

"Everything's under control," he announced to the room. There was some grumbling but overall everyone seemed to be satisfied with his words. I wondered how they could just trust him like that, although they didn't realize how many navy men were outside the door. Then the old man beckoned to Richard and me saying, "Come on lads. Let's talk."

He had a heavy limp in his right leg, causing him to lurch with every step. We followed him to an empty table in the corner but continued to stand as he sat down. He seemed unfazed by our lack of trust, leaning back, crossing his arms, and calling across the room for the bartender to bring over three drinks. He didn't specify what kind, and the bartender didn't ask.

"Shouldn't we be trying to get out of here?" I said slowly.

The old man waved a hand at the table. "Sit down, relax a minute."

I glanced at Richard. "How are we supposed to relax when the navy is just outside…?"

The man sat up, suddenly serious. "Keep your voices down and listen. The navy is either going to wait until you try to leave, or they're going to storm this place. But until they decide which option to take, and until they prepare to take it, we have ourselves some time to talk."

I thought about what to do. Most of me was anxious to just run out the door. I knew it was a sure way to get caught, but the urge to get out of the tavern was there. I think what kept me from doing it was my interest in this man, as well as the logic he had just given me. We had never met him before, yet the first moment he saw us, he gave us refuge. And now, with the navy just outside, all he wanted to do was talk. Or, at least so he claimed.

I sat down, nodding to Richard so he would follow my lead. The bartender brought over three glasses filled with some sort of ginger alcohol. The old man seemed pleased with my decision and raised a glass. Richard and I followed suit.

"Cheers, lads." He downed the entire drink in one large, gulp. Richard also drank all of his, but it took him longer. I, on the other hand, took just a sip and immediately my throat seemed be set aflame, tears springing to my eyes. I coughed pathetically.

"What is this?" I croaked, setting my glass down and pushing it away.

"Bourbon!" he said with a hearty laugh.

When I could see clearly again, I looked at him closely. I realized that he wasn't as old as I had initially thought, and that to call him an old man was actually an injustice. Sure, his hands were wrinkled and gnarled and so was his face, and his beard was mostly gray, but his eyes held a hint of youth and the hair atop his head was full and brown. Sure, he seemed bent and worn, but his chin remained lifted and his muscles were strong. Even as I studied him, I saw that he was doing the same to me. I wondered what he saw.

"Who are you?" I said at last.

The man's eyes narrowed but there was also a gentle smirk on his face. "My name is Philip Reuben. And who are you?"

"I'm Stephen Boswell and this is Richard Titus."

"That navy man only mentioned one criminal. Which of you is the one?" The man kept his eyes on me as he asked this. I knew that he already knew it was me, but I admitted it to him anyway. I expected him to ask what I did, but instead he asked what part Richard played in this.

"I helped Stephen escape," Richard replied.

Philip Reuben nodded slowly. He seemed to be thinking although I couldn't have guessed what. Still, he gazed at me.

"How old are you, lad?"

"Twenty-three," I answered.

"You did more than desert. Didn't you?"

His question stunned me, not just from its sudden obtrusiveness, but also from its accuracy. Still, he didn't come right out and ask what I had done. Yet I was certain that's what he wanted to know. So I told him.

"I killed the commodore."

Putting it into words for the first time made the whole thing seem suddenly much more real. While I didn't feel proud or accomplished, I strangely also didn't feel guilty. What hurt me the most was the knowledge that Jane had just lost her father and didn't even know it yet, and I was to blame. Oddly, even that knowledge didn't weigh on me much. While at the time I thought that I wasn't feeling anything, I know now that I was too confused to realize that I was feeling anger.

After everything the navy had done to me, now it had turned me into a killer. While in the past I may have wallowed in self-pity and tortured wonderment as to why this was happening to me, I now saw it as a chance to turn the tables. I had tried to be an exemplary sailor, to give those above me all that they wanted. Yet my best wasn't good enough. It never would be. And it was dictated from my birth. I'd never be able to do anything about it.

Except now I could. Now I had an opportunity to fight back, to free myself. I may have escaped from my role within their hierarchy, but they still surrounded me, quite literally. To be truly free I would need to act. Killing the commodore opened up an opportunity. Coming to terms with my deed opened up the realization.

I suddenly understood everything my father had been trying to tell me.

And I knew what I had to do.

CHAPTER TWENTY-EIGHT

CAPTAIN BOSWELL GAVE HIS ORDERS; to travel north and attack the next ship they saw, no matter what it was. The pirates glanced at each other, unnerved. The next ship appeared soon enough. It was a slaver.

Titus tried to reason. "That ship isn't worth taking, Stephen. We should wait for the next."

Captain Boswell's voice was unsettling. "No. We are taking that ship."

"Would you stop and think for a moment? What is the point in taking a slaver?"

"I am thinking!" Captain Boswell snapped, his voice dangerous. "I'm thinking that the British are right behind us and we need to travel as far and as fast as possible without stopping lest they catch us. I'm thinking that we need to restock our food lest we run out before we are safely away and are forced to stop, giving the British a chance to catch us. And I'm thinking that we have no idea when we'll run into another ship, but we have one right here in front of us. Now get the men battle-ready and take that ship!"

Alice dutifully went into the cabin before the killing started without needing to be told. She had heard the exchange between the two men and feared for Captain Boswell. She feared for his morality, for his humanity.

The *Vengeance Dragon* approached the other ship easily. The other crew was quite large yet unprepared for a battle. They were armed, but only to quell rebellion from within the ship, not to fend off an attack from the outside.

The *Vengeance Dragon* halted the other ship with chain shots, destroying the masts and rudder. Under the shadow of the red flag, the pirates boarded the slaver, issuing wild cries and hacking away at everyone who stood in their way. Some of the slavers simply dropped their weapons, surrendering, only to be cut down anyway. No one was left alive, not even a few to taunt as was customary.

The entire takeover of the ship took just minutes. Then some of the pirates went below deck. They returned immediately, their hands covering their noses and mouths. One vomited.

Avery Addison walked passed them all with a purposeful stride. He started toward the hatch that would lead below, but Captain Boswell put a hand on his chest to stop him.

"Are you sure you want to go down there?" he asked sternly.

"If those are my people down there," Addison said just as sternly, holding a steady, unwavering gaze with the captain, "then I must see them for myself."

Captain Boswell didn't say anything, but he removed his hand and allowed Addison to go below. Then he and Titus followed.

The three were met with a putrid stench of unkempt and unclean bodies. Before they had even gone all the way down the stairs, before they could even see any of the imprisoned Africans, the smell reached them first. By the time they reached the bottom of the stairs, they each had a hand covering their noses.

Row upon row, stack upon stack, of people, all chained hand and foot, all lying within suffocating confines, all looking at the three men that had come down to look at them. It was difficult to distinguish each person in the dark; there were no lights of any kind below this deck and the people were already so dark to begin with. The more their eyes adjusted to the darkness, the more Africans the pirates were able to see. Their presence seemed to never end. There must have been over a hundred of them.

Titus was only able to manage a minute or so. He mumbled something that neither Captain Boswell nor Addison could understand, or cared to understand under the current situation, and returned to the light. After a moment, Captain Boswell put a hand on Addison's shoulder and turned him back to the stairs so that they, too, could return.

Titus was oddly smiling very widely. "Do you know how much money we could get for those slaves? We should ship them to the colonies, sell them for a good price."

"No!" Addison shouted, a strange loud sound from a usually quiet man. "We must return them home. There's no question about it."

"And waste this opportunity?" Titus rebuked, taking an intimidating step toward Addison. "We attacked for food, and this ship has plenty. But it has so much more."

A few men gave a cry of consent while others nodded enthusiastically. But there were still some that didn't seem sure.

"Please." Addison's voice had gone back to its low volume. "Think about what'll happen to them. I was a slave once, as you all know. They will spend the rest of their lives in hell, and so will their children. If they manage to escape, I doubt there will conveniently be a pirate ship waiting to give them their freedom."

The men fell silent as they remembered the day they met Addison, the day he appeared out of the darkness, frightened, hunted. He had given up much to join them. And now he was as much one of them as they were to each other.

Captain Boswell stepped in between Titus and Addison. He wore a grave expression. "We're not going to ransom them. You should know better, Titus. But we're also not going to bring them back. We need to get rid of them. Like we always do."

It seemed that a whole minute went by before the full meaning of the captain's words became realized. There was nothing but silence on the decks of the two ships during that time. Then there was an explosion of dissent, mostly from Titus and Addison.

"What a waste!" Titus shouted while Addison said more quietly, "Surely you aren't serious."

Captain Boswell did not back down. "If we ransom them we risk full exposure. If we bring them back then we have a hundred uncontrollable witnesses, not to mention slavers that will wonder why an entire village suddenly reappeared. Either way is too risky." He paused, eyeing Titus and Addison one at a time before continuing. "Don't forget the British are on our tail. We need to run. We have no other option."

When the captain finished, there was another moment of silence. Then Avery Addison suddenly became a different man. His face screwed into one of rage, his hands clenched. He looked as though he might lash out. Captain Boswell stood his ground, ready for Addison to do anything. Yet Addison did nothing.

"You are out of your mind," he said. Then he left the slaver, hopping the bulwarks to the *Vengeance Dragon*.

Captain Boswell turned his attention to the remaining pirates. "I don't expect any of you to help me. But this is something that must be done." He looked at Titus, kept his expression neutral. But couldn't keep the plea out of his eyes.

Titus turned his back, shaking his head in disbelief. He threw over his shoulder, "Addison is right. You are crazy."

All but two pirates walked with Titus back to the *Vengeance Dragon*. Hugh Clinton and Adrian Paine went with Captain Boswell below deck of the slaver. Adam Paisley started to follow but Clinton harshly told him to turn back. They used daggers to pry up planks from the bottom of the ship, letting it quickly fill with salty water. The slaves started to shout and rattle their chains, straining against their restraints and grabbing at the pirates if they got too close. A few managed to get loose, breaking their own wrists or finally getting through the chain that they had been working at for the many weeks out on the ocean, their desperation giving them a surge of energy. The pirates shot or stabbed each one of these escapees. One slave fled rather than attacked, but he hardly made it one step before he, too, fell to a bullet.

Once enough planks were pulled, the pirates waited until the water was knee high. Captain Boswell wanted to be sure that no more slaves would be able to get away before the ship had completely sunk. Then, with cries of terror in their ears, they returned to their own vessel.

As the *Vengeance Dragon* pulled away, the pirates gathered at its side to watch the slaver sink further and further into the deep blue. Alice was among them. The screams were audible. They filled her head. They were the same screams that had filled the *Sea Maiden* as a pirate ship bearing a red flag approached it. The same pirate ship carrying the captain that would kill her father without a thought, just as he was killing these slaves.

Alice saw Captain Boswell walk toward the cabin. He wore no emotion. It seemed that he saw nothing. Heard nothing. He wouldn't make eye contact with her. Alice wanted to shout at him. She wanted to turn him around, to push his face toward the sinking ship, to show him all the lives he was taking. She wanted him to understand what he was doing, to remind him what he had done to her when he took her father. But when Alice opened her mouth, she burst into sobbing. When the slaver was completely submerged, the screams ceased, but it didn't give her the relief she had been hoping for.

Someone led Alice to the other side of the ship. When they got there she saw that it was Jerome.

"Jerome... did he... why? I can't..." Alice sputtered around with words, starting to breathe heavily. Jerome calmed her down and she started again. "He killed them all. He drowned them, Jerome. I thought he had changed. But he's exactly the same as when... I don't know who he is. I don't know what I'm doing here."

Jerome didn't say anything. There was nothing he could think of. So he just stayed with her, giving her a meaningful silence and compassionate presence rather than empty words.

CHAPTER TWENTY-NINE

~ 1716, Summer ~

A S RICHARD, REUBEN, AND I SAT around the table in that criminal-infested tavern, the navy just outside the door, I made my resolution.

Rueben, still observing me, must have seen a change in my face, for he asked, "What are you thinking, lad?"

"I need a ship and a crew," I said, my voice steady with determination. Reuben's mouth spread into a smile. Oddly, it was a rather proud smile.

"I know how to get you both," he told me. "You'll have to be careful who you talk to, who you ask to join you. Going on the account is not easy, lad."

"And I can trust you?" I asked.

The question made his smile grow. "I'm a retired crewmember of *The Northern Ghost*, compensated for battle injuries that have since healed. Well, mostly."

"Compensated?" I repeated.

"Pirates aren't just free men, lad. We take care of each other. Ever heard of democracy? Consensus? The Code?"

I started to realize that my vision didn't exactly line up with what Reuben was telling me. While I strongly wanted to fight back against the navy and society, I considered my own personal safety to be priority. I knew that even with my own ship I would still be hunted. I wouldn't be able to make a single mistake lest I be found, and I wouldn't be able to let my crew make a mistake. My life depended on it.

Richard had been silent this whole time, and finally I turned to him. Yet he spoke before I could. "Are you certain that this is what you want to do, Stephen? It'll be dangerous and difficult and there won't be any going back."

"I'm certain, Richard. Do you remember when my father was killed? I started to understand... everything. And I think you were too. But now I really see. What else would I do? They will follow me everywhere..." I only stopped talking when Richard put a hand on my shoulder.

"I only wanted to make sure you were certain. Because I'm certain that I will support your decision. And I will support whatever you feel you need to do. I will follow you anywhere, Stephen."

I was touched. And then I asked him if he would be my first mate. He said of course.

"Remarkable," Reuben murmured. "But before you can have a first mate, you need to become a captain. You could steal a ship or you could pay for one. Both will be tricky in your current predicament."

I admitted to Reuben that neither Richard nor I had any money with us. And even if we did, it would be nowhere near enough to pay for an entire ship. I suggested selling the waterlogged gun that I had stolen from the ship, the gun that I had used to shoot the commodore. But Reuben said that it wasn't worth it, that I would be better off fixing it up and obtaining ammunition for it, as I might need it down the road.

We decided on a plan of thievery and bartering. It would be a long process, trading stolen ships for better ones, and working or stealing money to pay for the difference. We would also use this time to build connections with the help of Reuben and meet potential crewmembers, who we would need to rely on in order for us to avoid being caught, considering the navy was already after us.

"Just one problem," Richard pointed out. "How are we going to get out of this place?"

Reuben had an answer for that. Before escaping, he gave us directions to a pirate haven down the coast where he would meet us. It was territory that had been seized and was now controlled by pirates and would be safer than this area which simply had a pirate presence. Once there, we would regroup and get to work. Still, Reuben urged us to be cautious and not to speak to anyone until we were reunited with him. Men are greedy, he reminded us. Many would be willing to give up information on us if bribed.

Then Reuben told us to go upstairs and wait by one of the windows at the back of the building. We were to jump out the window when we heard the signal and make a run for it.

"What's the signal?" I asked expectantly.

Reuben beamed. "I'm gonna start a brawl, lads!" And he let out a laugh. We all stood and as Reuben made to walk away from us I took his arm, stopping him.

"Thank you, Reuben," I said. "And I'm sorry, but I have to wonder why you're doing all this to help us."

Reuben looked at me. It was a much more personal and invasive look than before. Yet I didn't feel uncomfortable. It was like he had already read me and now he was pondering what he had read.

"You've gone through a lot, I know that much," Reuben mused. "They call me an old man but my life is far from over. I've been living in this hole for too long...." We nodded to each other.

Richard and I made our way upstairs while Reuben hobbled to the front door. We stood ready by a back window, navy men standing just out of view below us. We heard a shout followed by a chorus of voices. The front door banged open. Chairs scraped across the floor. The men below us, hearing the commotion, charged through a back door, their weapons ready.

I went out the window first. Since Richard was the stronger of us, he held onto my forearms and lowered me as far as he could reach. I dropped the rest of the way, rolling not very gracefully as I landed. When Richard dropped, he pushed himself away from the building slightly and took the impact evenly between his feet and hands.

We ran. I could hear someone yelling, "Find Boswell!"

We had been prepared to walk the whole way to our destination. It would've taken half a day. Reuben knew a man with a boat in town. He was going to get there first and have somewhere to stay ready for us as we couldn't trust anyone.

When I saw a fishing boat moored nearby, and only one man by it, I decided to change our plan. I veered toward it, pulling Richard with me. He seemed to know what I was thinking as he didn't ask any questions, although his face revealed his skepticism.

My gun was not loaded. Even if it was, it would not have been able to shoot because of the water damage. I held it out anyway, pointing it at the man by the boat. His face turned white and he put his hands up.

"Untie the boat," I commanded. My voice was calm and cold. The man scrambled to comply, his fingers fumbling with the rope. "Hurry up!" I pressed the barrel to his face. I could see the sweat on his forehead. It gave me confidence.

When the boat was free, I shoved the man into the water. Richard pushed the boat away from the shore and we hopped in, each taking an oar.

"We seem to be off to a good start," Richard said. I could only agree. I felt very satisfied.

We met Reuben where he had told us to go. We arrived almost at the same time and the three of us entered the pirate haven together. The place was nothing short of a town, not unlike the one we had just left. However, there was no military presence. In fact, the town didn't even appear to belong to one country. As in the tavern we had just escaped, I saw people of all skin colors speaking all sorts of languages.

Reuben gave us a quick tour. He found us lodging and paid for it with his own money. It was a cheap single room on the second floor of a hostelry. Richard and I didn't mind the small space. In fact, I was just glad to sleep in a real bed again for the first time in many years.

As Richard and I settled down, finally fully catching our breath, Reuben spent the day collecting his money. He asked for his share from people he had invested with, he pried it from the people who had borrowed from him, and he cashed in on the people who owed him favors.

When he returned, the size of his purse was significant. Seeing all that money, I was eager for the next step. But Reuben told me to put it out of my mind for now. Instead, I should get a good night's sleep and think of nothing until tomorrow.

I did as he said. I slept for a long time, turning in before the sun had set. It was a restful and welcomed sleep. My legs and chest were sore the next morning, yet I hardly gave them any attention. I was only focused on getting to work.

CHAPTER THIRTY

ADDISON ENTERED THE CABIN. He didn't knock. Inside, Captain Boswell was sitting at his desk, but he wasn't doing anything. Just sitting. When Addison entered, the captain didn't bother to see who it was. He already knew.

"I can stay on this ship no longer," Addison told him firmly.

Captain Boswell nodded slowly. "I figured as much."

"All this time I thought you understood what it's like to lose your freedom." Addison had approached the desk. He stood tall, looking down on the seated captain. "You told me you had the scars on your back, do you remember that? Do you?"

"I do." Captain Boswell said it curtly, slightly cutting off Addison's last few words. He lifted his deep blue eyes to meet Addison's almost black ones.

"If you keep living like this then you'll never be free," Addison said. "You've forgotten your original purpose. You've gone so far astray that you can't even see it for yourself. I can't stay here."

"Do you know what that means?" Captain Boswell asked calmly.

"Yes."

"Do you want to die?" This question was just as calm as the first.

"No." Addison didn't let his gaze waver. "But I have always been willing to give up my life in order to be free. That's why I ran in the beginning. It's something you should understand."

Captain Boswell shook his head. "Life is more important to me."

"Then you'll forever be a slave. You may have escaped from the commodore, but you will never be free of him. You may have killed him, but even now he controls your life." Addison walked to the door. "I would prefer to leave sooner rather than later."

That same night, the *Vengeance Dragon* dropped anchor by a small, forested island. Captain Boswell and Addison went ashore by rowboat. The crew watched the two men disappear into the trees.

Alice urgently asked the few pirates that she was comfortable talking to what was going on. It was clear they knew by their solemn expressions, but they wouldn't tell her. She saw Titus gather and talk to a considerably large group of the men. Alice couldn't hear what he was saying but he repeatedly pointed at the helm. Some of the men were shaking their heads and others walked away. But the majority seemed interested in what he was saying. Ultimately an argument broke out and the group disbanded.

Everyone turned to the island when a single gunshot broke through the night. Captain Boswell returned a minute later. He was alone.

The *Vengeance Dragon* set out. Captain Boswell went straight into the cabin. The crew resumed their activities like any other night. Only they did so in near silence. The atmosphere of the ship did not feel like any other night.

Jerome wouldn't tell Alice anything, not even the next morning. She knew better than to ask the captain himself, and it was clear that he wasn't in a talking mood anyway. She finally sat down on a barrel in defeat. Reuben hobbled over next to her and, without even being asked, said,

"Addison didn't want to be a crewmember anymore. His parents were taken from their homeland and shipped over to the colonies. He was born a slave before joining this crew. After what happened yesterday, it was too hard for him to stay here anymore."

"So he left?" Alice asked innocently.

Reuben sighed. It was a shuddering, sad sigh. "Yes. He left."

CHAPTER THIRTY-ONE

~ 1719 ~

THREE YEARS LATER I STOOD on the deck of the *Vengeance Dragon*, fully modified and equipped as it is now, for the first time. It belonged to me and me alone. I owed nothing, only thanks to the people that had helped me, my debts to them paid.

My crew arrived moments later. They were the men I had gathered over the past three years, men who had helped me or that I had helped, now willing to serve me and to be bound by my strict code.

It was their first time on the *Vengeance Dragon* as well as my own. We had all been on the ship before, and even sailed it, but back then cannons had not lined its sides. Back then the hold had not contained more space for people than for cargo. Back then the prow had not been adorned with a dragon figurehead. Back then a red flag had not flown from the top of the mainmast.

After our first night in the pirate haven, the night we escaped from the navy, we got to work. Reuben's money was a start. We used it and the boat that Richard and I had stolen to buy a cutter, a single-masted boat. It was only a small upgrade from the fishing boat in terms of size, but it would be able to handle the water at a very high speed and give us a bit more room. We lived in it in order to avoid having to pay for a room. Reuben even cooked for us, explaining that he had experience after getting injured since cooking was all he was good for on a ship.

We left the haven a few days after arriving, knowing that it would be dangerous to stay in one place for too long. The navy had undoubtedly followed us there and would be planning how to arrest me, either through bribes or threats. As Reuben had told us before, we couldn't trust anyone.

The three of us sailed from place to place, travelling up and down the Atlantic, laboring in some way for money at each location that we docked at. I felt that I was reliving my life from before the navy had snatched me away, but this time I was working more for money than for food and shelter. This time, I didn't have to live it alone. Richard and Reuben stayed close to me. We spent a lot of time talking.

We also upgraded our cutter although doing so took long because we worked on it ourselves, scrapping together material and learning how to use it as we went.

Our struggle with the boat caught the attention of a carpenter, Adrian Paine. Although we didn't realize it yet, he would become our first crewmember. His business was failing in competition to others and he owed taxes that he both could not pay and did not believe that he should pay. I didn't give him the details of my plight, but I told him enough to make him understand how serious it was and how distrustful I was of others. He proved his worth and desire to join us by gathering only his essential belongings and abandoning everything else to leave with us. His woodworking skills indeed came to great use.

When the cutter was ready to sell, Reuben took care of the transaction in order to limit the amount of people to see and remember my face, and possibly offer information about if prompted.

This was how we passed those three years, buying and stealing ships, upgrading them, then trading them for better ones. Once we got into the desired size range, I was never satisfied with the ships we picked up. We got to a point where we no longer needed to work for money as we had begun to make a profit. For a short while we even had two ships. We probably spent more time looking for the perfect ship than we needed to, and I know I was to blame. Reuben informed me that ships I wanted to sell were sufficient, yet I didn't feel satisfied with any of them. None of them felt right to me.

Throughout this time we picked up more crewmembers, yet I still didn't think of them as such. It simply didn't occur to me. We met fellow deserters, like Hugh Clinton, who were willing to man the cannons; thieves, like Miles Oscar, who were eager to get off the streets; and craftsmen, like Adrian Paine, who brought with them their own unique skills. They went through the cycle of trading ships with us, some even lending their personal money for the cause.

As we picked up these men, Reuben informed me that I should start drawing up my own set of articles, rules for each man to sign, a contract to bind them. I finished writing them when we had gathered our first four men.

I made clear to the men the stakes, as well as what they would need to give up. I knew my rules were strict. Maybe even dictatorial. But I wanted them to be fair. I wouldn't force anyone to sign, and I would only ask very specific people to do so. I needed men who wouldn't be missed while on my ship, men who had nowhere else to be, men that could be killers.

On my ship, going on the account would be about more than taking revenge or being free. It would be about staying safe. And I was determined to protect myself, no matter the cost.

Here follows the code that I created:

1. *Every man shall be equal. Every man shall have an equal share of provisions. Every man shall use his share at his pleasure, unless during a ration, which will take place by necessity and by vote. Some prizes shall be traded for provisions. Every man shall have an equal vote. All significant affairs shall be decided by vote.*

2. *If a man harms another man's body or provisions, or if he takes from another man's provisions, he shall have the right to explain his case, by which the crew shall vote on the necessity of punishment, and subsequently on the type of punishment.*

3. *Disputes shall be settled in a non-violent manner. If both parties cannot come to an agreement, a higher*

ranking man shall act as a mediator. If violence
ensues without resolution, one or both parties may be
subject to punishment, as voted upon by the crew.

4. No flogging, under any circumstance, shall take place
in this Company.

5. Every man to sustain an injury shall receive
compensation proportional to the injury as voted upon
by the crew.

6. Every man, to the best of his ability, shall perform
his duty and stay true to the Company and Captain.
He shall keep battle-ready and keep neat his body
and provisions. He shall commit to keeping the
Captain hidden from the Royal Navy.

7. The ship shall sail under a red flag. No quarter shall
be given. All persons of an enemy ship shall be killed.
Any ship which holds loyalty to any nation shall be
deemed an enemy.

8. No man shall leave the service of the Captain except
through death. No man shall leave the ship without
the Captain's consent. No man shall participate in
any action or speak to any person that may
jeopardize the safety of the Company and Captain.

9. *For the purpose of keeping order, the Captain shall*
    have the final say in all matters and shall issue orders
    as he sees fit. The Captain shall elect others of the
    Company to high ranking positions.

Adrian Paine, Charles Mather, Oliver Griffith, and High Clinton became the first to give me their signatures and their lives.

In time we obtained a full crew, and Reuben cooked for all of them. Nathaniel Penn, Isaac Owen, Adam Paisley, Miles Oscar, and Francis Wesley, among others, all signed the Articles. All of them were either from Britain or the British colonies. I didn't trust anyone that spoke a language other than English. They weren't as willing to be bound by my rules, anyway. Not as willing as my British men who held the same grudge against British society as I, something foreigners could not relate to.

When it came time to careen for the first time, we chose an island based on its size and location. It was inhabited by Caribbean natives, but I was able to give them weapons in exchange for permission to use their beach. They were as wary of strangers as I was, and they seemed to know it, only trusting me because of our common enemy. The more we beached on their island, the more our familiarity grew.

And then I met Avery Addison. He was a black man, an escaped slave. Our journey up the Atlantic coincidentally coincided with his escape north from the southern colonies. Anytime we docked, we waited until night to do so. Avery and his runaway companions had the same idea, keeping their movements contained to darkness. The dock is where I met them.

When Avery and I suddenly came face to face as I left the ship, we both froze out of panic, staring at each other. He thought I was a bounty hunter and that I would turn him in. I thought my cover had been blown and that he would do the same to me. Yet we slowly realized that we were no threat to each other. My crew revealed themselves to Avery, leaning over the side of the ship, and Avery's companions revealed themselves to me, emerging from the shadows. There were five of them in total.

I wanted to help them. The terror and the prey-like distrustfulness that I saw in their eyes was not unfamiliar. They asked for passage on my ship. I couldn't give it. I wouldn't be able to let them get off once they got on. It was a risk just to talk to them at all. Had I not felt for them, had they been anyone other than escaped slaves, I would have killed all five of them. Instead I offered to let them join me. They seemed to consider it. Until I told them my stipulations.

Avery shook his head, speaking for his group. "You would take our lives?"

"It's safety," I tried to reason.

"It's slavery."

"They joined willingly," I said. "What I can give them is worth more than what they gave up to be here."

"And what's that?" Avery sounded doubtful but curious.

"I can give them food, shelter. Equality. Vengeance." Avery said nothing. I continued. "We protect each other. I share their fate. In exchange for their lives, I am trusting them with mine."

"You are scared," Avery cautioned. "You are running, but do you know what it's like to be chased, hunted? To escape a life of pain and torment, one where you never know if the next day will be your last? Wishing it would end? And when it finally does, always having to look over your shoulder because at any time you could be pulled back into it, or worse?"

I was very aware of my crew listening to those words and was slightly self-conscious to reply, "I do know it."

There was silence. And then Avery asked if I had the scars to prove it as he did.

"I have the scars," I told him quietly. "I'm certain my experiences can't compare with yours, but I have the scars."

Avery thought. I could almost see his mind working. The others were shaking their heads. I assumed they were doing so because they weren't satisfied by anything I had said. It turns out they had predicted what Avery would say next and were already disagreeing with it.

"Do you consider yourself a free man?" he asked. I nodded. He asked if I was sure. I nodded again. "Then I'll join you."

When I presented Avery with the Articles to sign, he admitted that he had neither a surname nor any idea of how to write. And so I told him truthfully that this ship did not sail for any nation and that our laws were independent from all other. If he chose a last name here, it would be honored and it would be his regardless of the lack of recognition that nations would give it. Avery chose the surname of the man his mother desired to marry but had been legally banned from doing so due to her slave status; Addison.

I wrote down the name and Avery copied the letters in his own hand onto the Articles. His signature was crude and sloppy at best, but that didn't matter. When it was done, Mr. Addison shook my hand.

After finishing our business inland and departing, Addison and I spent several hours conversing in private. We shared our experiences, among other things. Besides Richard and Reuben, he came to know more about me and my past than anyone else on my ship. I gave him the role of sail maker as he had spent some time apprenticed to a tailor before being sold as a field hand.

Addison was with us when we felt confident enough to attack a ship for the first time out in open waters. I was curious to test the competency of my men in combat, as well as the effectiveness of our various weapons. I was also curious about myself. I had only killed one man, the commodore.

We chose a small merchant ship with a crew half the size of our own to attack. Our cannons destroyed the rudder and sails easily enough. Then we boarded and killed crewmembers until they surrendered.

The survivors knelt in a line and my men stood in front of them, ready to kill. They all knew before we had started that our career as pirates would be one without mercy. Yet they looked at me, waiting for my permission, I suppose, or perhaps giving me a chance to make sure this was what I really wanted.

I glanced at the flag that towered over us all from the top of my ship. Red. The color of blood. I approached the nearest kneeling man. His face was tear streaked. I pulled out my pistol, now repaired as Reuben had suggested on the day I met him. I pressed the barrel to the man's forehead and fired. The back of his head seemed to burst. I watched it happen. I felt nothing as he died. Gunshots echoed mine as my men killed the rest.

We took all of the cargo. I personally explored the captain's cabin. I was drawn immediately to a wooden box sitting on a table square in the middle of the room. The box was long and made of fine wood, stained a rich, deep brown. I knew what was inside and delicately lifted the lid. A rapier. Not a foil as used by the naval officers for sport that I had so often admired. The blade was thicker than that of a foil, the tip sharper, and the sword as a whole much heavier. Its hilt was of a simple design, with a cup-shaped handguard, typical of Spanish design, and a black grip. I carefully raised it out of the box and drew the sword a few inches out of its sheath. The metal of the blade was polished and its edge was sharp. I buckled the sword to my waist.

When I turned around, Richard was in the doorway, watching me. He said, "That sword is impractical for…." He trailed off at the patronized look I gave him. He was silent for just a moment, and then with sincerity said, "That sword suits you."

Once the entire ship had been pillaged, we sunk it. Cheers erupted from the crew, our first raid successful. That day, a precedent was set. The steps we would take after forcing a crew to surrender would resemble those that we took as I have recounted. Always, I would lead.

Then finally, during the year 1719, I obtained and completed renovating and stocking my perfect ship. Her final touch was a dragon figurehead, carved by Paine and guided by the imagination of several crewmembers. I named her the *Vengeance Dragon*. The name came easily to me.

In the presence of my crew, thirty-five of them in total, Reuben approached me.

"Stephen," he said. "There is one thing I wish to ask of you. And that would be permission to sign your code, if you will have me, Captain."

"Of course I will have you," I replied.

All this time Reuben had remained in a position of power above me. He was the one with the experience, the knowledge, the plans to make all this happen. I never felt threatened by this. Quite the opposite. Yet I had never thought that I would hear him use my title or want to be bound by my rules, and I certainly was not going to ask him to. With a stroke of a quill, Reuben stepped down below me.

Then Richard met my eye and, knowing what he was thinking, I shook my head. He took the quill anyway.

"You don't have to do this," I nearly whispered.

"It wouldn't be fair if I didn't. We're meant to stand against everything that ever hurt us. That includes unfairness." As he signed, I knew he was right. He continued, "Besides. I said I would support you. I still intend to do so."

The names came to total thirty-eight. Including my own.

A few months later we picked up Jerome Wistar. He was a fiddler that hid while we killed everyone on his ship. We were surprised to find him just before sinking the ship. Seeing use in his ability to entertain and after learning of his bad experiences with the crew we had just killed, I offered him to join us. He readily agreed, especially since the only alternative was death. Because of the unusual circumstance by which he joined, and our lack of expectation for him to help us kill others, he was exempt from signing the Articles. Every man voted on this and it was unanimous. He would still be expected to follow our basic rules. In return, he would be protected.

A tenth and final point was added to the Articles:

> 10. *The musician's only task is to play his instrument. He shall play by request and as he pleases. He shall cease playing if asked. He may refuse a request if he feels he has sufficiently played during that day. The Company shall keep the musician safe from harm.*

It was then that I felt complete. While I was still running from the navy, I no longer had to search for a sense of stability. I had sought a ship and a crew. I had found a home and a family. All I had to do now was survive.

CHAPTER THIRTY-TWO

ALICE NEEDED TO KNOW. She needed to know just who Captain Boswell was. Not the pirate, but the man. Surely there was an explanation for... everything.

She scoured his things. He had so many papers, so many writings, there had to be something on his past. She had looked through his papers before, but this time she was searching through them. There was a difference. It mattered to her.

Alice went into his bedroom. She rifled through the shelf of bound books, rummaged through his chest. Nothing. But she was sure. He was that kind of person, someone who wrote everything down.

She stood in the center of the room, her hands on her hips, and scanned the area. The frame of the bed, at the base. Was that a loose panel? Alice knelt and stuck her fingers around the edges. She pulled. It came free. The area inside was small. Just large enough to hold...

A leather-bound journal. She had found it.

Alice hurriedly replaced the panel and dashed back to her own room. She sat on the bed, leaned against the wall, and crossed her legs in front of her. She opened the journal and read. She read for hours straight.

She found her answer. And she also found that she knew a very important secret that no one else on the ship knew. But she didn't get to read the whole journal, for a commotion outside interrupted her.

She tossed the journal aside onto her bed and ran out of the cabin to see what the matter was. The men had abandoned their duties and gathered on the main deck, jostling each other and shouting. Two were at the center, their noses bloody, and they were being held back by the others.

A fight, Alice realized. She had come out at the tail end of it. She saw Captain Boswell put a hand on the chest of one of the men and push him away. He spoke a few words to him, and the man seemed to immediately lose his aggression, bowing his head and slumping his shoulders. Then he spoke to the other man, but this time his words had less of an effect. This man was not as ready to calm down. He stormed away, sweeping a hand through the air.

The crowd dispersed and slowly returned to work. Titus stood by. He had watched the entire encounter and done nothing to intervene. Now he walked after the aggressor and they exchanged words.

Alice let out a breath, not realizing how tense she had been during the skirmish. She was impressed by Captain

Boswell's ability to resolve it so quickly. Yet even now she could feel the tension among the men and knew that whatever they had fought about had not truly been resolved, and this knowledge frightened her. As she stood and watched the dispute blow over, she thought of the Articles she had just read. And then she thought of everything she had just read, all of the captain's past.

She needed to talk to someone. Anyone. She stood still and swept the ship with her eyes, searching for Reuben. He had always been easy to talk to. But he was currently standing near the captain, who had gone down by the prow.

Alice pleaded in her mind for Reuben to look her way. *Come on, come on*, she thought. His eyes lifted. She quickly beckoned. Reuben smiled and submitted to her, his bad leg dragging across the deck as he came.

"Alright, little lady?" he asked.

"Mister Reuben, can I talk to you?"

"When I said anytime, I meant it."

"It's about the captain," she said, in a way asking for permission to discuss the man. Reuben simply gave a nod. Alice took a deep breath and let it spill before she could change her mind. "I found Captain Boswell's journal and I read it and before you say anything, please, can you just help me to understand why you helped him all those years ago and why you're still helping him? Surely you've seen him change. I mean, from what I've read about him, he was a *completely* different person back then."

Reuben lifted his eyebrows and put a hand up to make Alice slow down. She stopped talking and looked at him earnestly.

"Is this what's been on your mind, little lady?"

Alice nodded. "I'm just, I'm very bothered by all that's happened, Mister Reuben. And you've been with him the longest except for Titus. Did you know he wanted to sail under the red flag when you helped him?"

"I didn't know, but I worried." Reuben sighed. "I helped him in the beginning because I felt sorry for the lad. He had been through a lot, that much was clear. But he also had resolve. I believed him to be a true leader, capable of being a great captain. In fact, I still do. He put purpose back into my life." Reuben shook his head. "Then he wrote those Articles and hoisted the red flag up his mast. Part of me still believed in him. Part of me was concerned. He had earned my respect for sure, but I also wanted to watch over him. I joined his crew for both those reasons."

"You care about him."

Reuben let out a little laugh. It held more rumination than humor. "Yes, I suppose you're right there, little lady. He was just a lad when I met him. I've watched him grow. And I've watched him regress."

Alice shifted her weight, uncomfortable at imagining Captain Boswell as a young man. Even as she had read his journal, she had pictured him as he was now.

"What changed?" she asked.

Reuben thought very carefully, even rubbing his bearded chin. "I think he got caught up in this pirate life. All of the killing, it took him over. He lost the ability to empathize. When you came, I was so scared for you. So scared. This rule he had created about leaving no one alive, it had been about survival. But now, sometimes I fear that he is killing simply for the sake of killing."

"It's his fear," Alice pointed out. "I heard it from Jerome. He's terrified of being caught and he'll do anything to prevent that from happening."

"He's terrified of death," Reuben corrected. "That privateer, Captain Gandy, had said so, and he had meant it as an insult, an exaggeration. He didn't know he was speaking the truth. Captain Boswell's fear has consumed him."

"So why let him continue like this, Mister Reuben? He trusts you. In fact, he thinks very highly of you. You should talk to him, put an end to this. He'll listen to you."

Reuben's voice rose, like waking from a sleepwalk. "No!" He turned his face to the sea and breathed. "I'm afraid I don't have it in me. Weak, I know, but true. I wouldn't be able to face him like that. In the end, I chose to follow him, and if I could go back, knowing what I do now, I would do it all over again, even if just to be with him. But *you*, little lady, are a different story."

Alice drew back, dazed. "Me?"

"Yes, little lady." He softened his voice and bowed his head, looking down at her solemnly. "The captain hasn't just spared your life, Miss Bradford. He has been protecting it. And that has to mean something. I can't say where we'll all end up or what will become of us, but even if nothing comes of it, it has to mean something. And that matters."

Alice was awestruck. She had no reply. Reuben patted her shoulder reassuringly and started to leave.

"Wait, Mister Reuben!"

The older man paused. His eyes twinkled.

"I need to tell you that I'm…" Alice slowed her words. Should she tell him? Of everyone on this ship, shouldn't it be him? But why did it have to be anyone at all? "I'm sorry if I bothered you with my questions."

The crow's feet around Reuben's eyes deepened as he smiled. "Not at all, Miss Bradford." And he left.

Alice blew out a breath. She still wasn't sure if she had made the right choice, if she should have let Reuben in on her secret. Yet there was no time to dwell on it as a shadow moved down the steps of the quarterdeck. Titus rounded on Alice, a mountain towering over her small frame.

"Reuben doesn't know a damn thing he's talking about," he growled at her.

Alice, unnerved, shakily asked as politely as she could, "Whatever do you mean, sir?"

"Whatever do you mean, sir?" he mocked, imitating her posh English accent. "Your presence don't mean a thing to the captain. He's gone to shit. He needs to be stopped."

Alice was taken aback by Titus' foul language. She thought she'd better leave him, and quickly. However, even as she thought this, he came a little closer and peered at her with an interrogating eye.

"Did you recognize the name Benjamin Madison before?"

Alice swallowed and found it difficult. "No."

Titus pointed a threatening finger at her. "I know you're hiding something, *Miss Bradford*, and I'm reasonably sure I know what it is. But don't worry, I won't tell a soul." He stuck his face uncomfortably close to hers and she could feel his breath on her skin as he spoke. "Just remember, the captain doesn't care about you. Not really. You're nothing to him."

He abruptly strode away, leaving Alice shaking. She didn't understand what any of that was supposed to mean, and it disturbed her. Perhaps she and Reuben should have discussed him more than the captain, for wasn't it true that he had changed as well?

Titus walked slowly with strong steps down the ship, not in any hurry. He noted the mist that was rolling in. Soon it would entirely swallow the *Vengeance Dragon*. Captain Boswell approached, done with his business at the prow and returning to his cabin. Titus squared his shoulder and the two men bumped. Captain Boswell took the impact to his injured arm and he winced.

"You better watch out, Stephen," Titus spat, whirling around.

Captain Boswell took a step back. "Richard...?"

"I mean it." Titus kept walking without another word, faster this time.

Captain Boswell looked after him, troubled, before he too continued his walk.

CHAPTER THIRTY-THREE

CAPTAIN BOSWELL RETURNED TO HIS CABIN and Alice stayed close by, feeling for some odd reason that she should be with him. Looking at him now, knowing everything that had happened to him in the past, it was as if he wore a mask, and it made her sad. Did she truly have it in her to feel compassion for him?

He glanced up, saw her watching him. Asked if she was alright.

"Yes."

And she moved closer, asked what he was doing and if she could help. The mist outside had blocked the sun, darkening the cabin. He asked for a lamp, and she brought him a handheld one. He smiled a little. She had never seen him do that before.

It didn't last long. They heard a gunshot. And then they felt the *Vengeance Dragon* slow to a dead stop.

Captain Boswell stood, his chair scraping across the wood. He moved to the door with some speed. Opened it. Hardly had time to step out when someone who had been waiting for him swung a block of wood at his head.

Alice cried out something indistinguishable as the captain flew back and crashed to the floor, both hands clutching at his forehead. Alice covered her mouth in shock.

The pirate with the wood dropped his makeshift weapon. There was a splat of blood on it. He entered the cabin with another, Oliver Griffith. They momentarily blinked at Alice, seemingly with uncertainty. Then they each took one of Captain Boswell's arms. They hauled him up and dragged him out. Captain Boswell let them take him without giving resistance.

Alice could feel her heart beating in her chest. She felt it might explode out of her body, or rise up into her throat. She forced herself forward, taking each step with some effort, until she came to stand in the doorway and could see out on the deck.

Hugh Clinton was dead. He laid in a heap, blood spreading from his chest. Adam Paisley stood over him, still holding the pistol that he had used to kill his senior. His face was pale, his eyes were wet. He stared down, feeling sick, unable to move.

Philip Reuben, Isaac Owen, Francis Wesley, and a few others had been disarmed, their swords and guns lying in a pile. Three pirates stood a few paces away from them, aiming pistols. Others, including Nathaniel Penn and Charles Mather, still had their weapons, but were under similar guard, although less blatantly. Their eyes darted between the two groups, apparently on the fence about the divide. Adrian Paine stood off to the side, alone, his arms crossed, his face betraying no emotion.

Jerome sidled up next to Alice. He said nothing, just put his arm around her shoulders and held her tight. One sob escaped her.

Griffith and the other pirate brought Captain Boswell to the center of the ship where Titus was waiting. The former first mate unbuckled Captain Boswell's sword belt and removed the rapier from his waist, holding onto it firmly. His face was like stone.

"We've decided that you are no longer fit to be captain," Titus said loudly. "We're putting an end to this madness."

"Are you crazy? The navy is right-"

"*I am done* with all this navy nonsense, Stephen. I am tired and fed up with your paranoid obsession, and so are the men."

Captain Boswell tried to reason with logic, his voice straining. "I have been trying to keep us alive, Richard. Everything I've done has been for the safety of our crew."

"What you've done makes me feel like I'm in the navy again!" Titus barked. Captain Boswell opened his mouth to speak, but Titus never gave him a chance. After shouting, "Shut up!" he struck Captain Boswell's face with the hilt of the rapier.

Alice flinched. The men stiffened. Adrian Paine uncrossed his arms. He marched toward Titus.

Captain Boswell saw him coming. "No. No, don't. Don't!"

Titus turned to face Paine. Paine drew back his fist, ignoring Captain Boswell. Titus pointed a pistol at Paine's nose and fired. The back of Paine's head exploded and his body collapsed.

Captain Boswell closed his eyes. "My God, Richard, what are you doing?"

"No, you don't get to say that." Titus made a shooing gesture. "Tie him to the mast."

The pirates pushed Captain Boswell's back up against the mast and wrapped coarse rope over his chest, securing him. He didn't resist. In fact, he made it quite easy for them. The only sign of defiance he showed was to glare continuously at Titus.

"What will you do now?" he asked when it was done. "This is where your plan stops, isn't it? You haven't thought beyond this point."

Titus wiggled his jaw, pondering. He jerked his head at the two pirates and they cleared away. Titus stepped forward. He and Captain Boswell were now at a conversational distance from each other.

"If you want to say something, then say it." Titus spoke low enough so no one else could hear.

Captain Boswell softened his gaze. "Why didn't you come to me? We could have talked."

Titus was already shaking his head. "I don't know how to talk to you anymore, Stephen. I've brought it up before, but you never listened. I'm sorry it had to come to this. You're just so stuck to your ways, so blind…."

Titus trailed off. He leaned back, thinking. Captain Boswell watched him, unsure of what to make of this display. Titus swept his eyes around the ship until they found Alice and came to rest on her face. Alice froze under his gaze. Captain Boswell looked back and forth between the two of them, suddenly worried.

"Alice, come here," Titus said, his hand extended. His words weren't harsh, but they weren't kind either. Alice shrunk back, trying to burrow herself into Jerome's arm.

"I said come here!" Titus bellowed.

He stomped over to her and snatched up her arm, pulling her easily out of Jerome's feeble grip. Reuben stiffened and he would have moved forward if not for Owen putting his arm out, stopping him from doing anything rash. Titus dragged Alice to the captain. She pulled away but it hardly made a difference.

Captain Boswell pressed against his restraints. "Don't you dare hurt her, Richard."

"Oh, I would never hurt her. Do you know why? No, of course you don't, you blind, ignorant fool. Look at her." Titus held Alice still against his chest. The rapier was still in his hand, sheathed, and he pressed it against her. To him, it was simply in the way. To others, it looked like a threat. "Look at her!"

Captain Boswell snapped his eyes to Alice, not at all understanding what this was about, but not wanting to disobey. Alice stared at his boots.

"Even now you don't see it," Titus said with a hint of mockery and disappointed amazement. "It didn't take me long at all. But you. I am so surprised at you." He gave Alice a slight shake. "Tell him your mother's name. Go on, tell him."

Alice slowly lifted her eyes like she was about to betray him. And as she said it, her eyes glistened with tears.

"Jane Bradford."

"And her maiden name. Go on."

"Madison."

And just like that, Captain Boswell saw it. He saw the resemblance, the tinge of red in her hair, the bright blue eyes, and he wondered how he had never noticed it before, how it had never even occurred to him before. It pained him terribly. He couldn't look her in the eye. Not after all he had put her through. He sagged, held up only by the ropes that bound him.

Alice watched Captain Boswell transform into a broken, defeated man right in front of her. She saw his eyes well up.

Behind the captain, she saw a large ship emerge from the mist. It sailed right into the *Vengeance Dragon* with a crash, rocking the little pirate ship violently and knocking several men off their feet. Titus lost his grip on Alice and she scrambled away from him. Two more ships appeared and they closed in. All three flew Union Jacks.

CHAPTER THIRY-FOUR

GUNSHOTS FILLED THE AIR as navy men boarded the *Vengeance Dragon*. All around Alice, men fell dead. Some dashed for their weapons but hardly had a chance to fight back. Others jumped overboard. This included Titus who didn't even give a backward glance. While some managed to swim, others drowned.

Alice didn't think. She only reacted and picked up a dropped knife and started sawing away at the bonds securing Captain Boswell. She focused on nothing else. Once the rope was cut, Captain Boswell started to slide down the mast to the deck, but Alice grabbed him and kept him from falling. He still wouldn't look at her.

"Captain, please." Her voice broke and she could feel the tears threatening her, but she planted herself in front of Captain Boswell, forcing herself to be strong. "Please."

He finally looked at her. His eyebrows were scrunched up, his eyes lifeless and wet. "Alice, I..."

"Come on!" She pulled on him and he seemed to snap to reality, taking in the British warships. Now his eyes went wide and he became struck with terror. Alice repeated, "Come on!"

Finally, he got moving. He seemed to suddenly be set with resolve, picking up a pair of pistols and jogging to the cabin.

"What are you doing!" Alice cried helplessly as she followed.

"I need to do this."

When they were both inside, he pushed the desk against the door, barring it closed. Then with trembling hands he rummaged through the documents on a shelf, chaotically tossing paper over his shoulder now and then until he found what he was looking for.

"Alice, will you bring a lamp here, please?"

Alice obeyed, retrieving the handheld lamp that was still lit from earlier. It cast an eerie glow around the cabin. Captain Boswell held the paper he had been looking for over the flame. It was the Articles.

"This has the name of every crewmember on this ship," he explained solemnly as the list took to burning. "No one would be safe if the British got it."

The fire licked up the paper greedily. When it had nearly reached his fingertips, the captain dropped it and stomped the flames out with his boot. The deed was done. The navy was coming. Their footsteps resounded on the wood of the deck. Captain Boswell swallowed his panic. He could do nothing else to hide his fear.

"They're going to come in here." Even his voice shook. He kept his back to her. "Alice, your mother-"

"You don't need to say anything," she interrupted.

He gave a small nod of acknowledgment. Then he nearly whispered, "They can take you to her."

She stared wide-eyed at his back, the prospect of being reunited with her mother moving her. It was what she wanted, more than anything.

Captain Boswell lifted his two pistols, aiming them at the door. "Alice, you need to go in your room and get on the floor. Keep the door open. Try to be still."

Alice did as she was told. They waited. She could hear the captain's breathing, heavy and uneven. Should she say something to him? To calm him, or reassure him, or to... say goodbye? She never got the chance to decide.

They navy men pushed on the door. The desk skidded. As soon as he saw a body, Captain Boswell fired a shot. The men retreated momentarily and then returned with more force. The door flew open, the desk pushed away. Captain Boswell fired his second shot. The lead man fell. The others stepped over him, five of them. Captain Boswell dropped his pistols and picked up his chair in a last desperate attempt. He swung it, knocking one man aside. The others barreled into him. They tackled him down. They tried to restrain him. He resisted wildly.

Alice covered her ears as the navy men resorted to kicking Captain Boswell. Each impact resounded with a heavy thud, sending vibrations through the floor. Alice cringed. The beating didn't last long. Just long enough to make the captain stop his struggling.

One of the navy men approached Alice with caution. He held a rifle and pointed it at her. She put her hands in the air, tears streaking down her face, and the man quickly put it down, squatting in front of her.

"Everything's going to be okay, miss," he said kindly. His accent. It was so English. He gave her a hand and she readily took it.

He guided her out, passed Captain Boswell who was on his knees, bent forward in pain, his hands being tied behind his back, his chest heaving.

Out on the main deck, so many pirates has been killed. Their bodies lay sprawled about. Alice couldn't tell who was among them, and she had no idea who had escaped. She was led past in a daze.

Jerome was alive. He didn't have his fiddle with him. Some navy men were questioning him. Alice briefly heard him say, "No, no, it's written somewhere. It says in the log, 'the musician is a captive' and 'the musician did not sign the Articles.' That's me, I'm the musician."

Alice was brought to Jerome. His face lit up when he saw her with relief.

"Are you okay, Alice?"

Alice hurried to his side and he wrapped his arm around her.

"Are you two together?" one man asked.

"Yes. Well, no." Jerome explained, "We met on this ship. We're both captives."

"Is this true?" the man asked Alice gently. She nodded, not trusting her voice. "And can you tell me your name, miss?"

Alice squeaked, "Alice Bradford."

"Alice Bradford!" they each exclaimed, and one gestured toward the larger of the three navy ships. "I beg your pardon, miss. Let's get you off this pirate vessel."

Alice kept her eyes locked ahead, afraid to catch a glimpse of any of the dead bodies. She walked with Jerome and the sailors up a gangplank and onto a warship twice the size of the *Vengeance Dragon*. Alice hardly noticed it. They brought her to the cabin and asked her to wait. Benjamin Madison would see her soon. Jerome wasn't allowed inside. This cabin was fancy, almost too fancy, with elaborate books lining beautifully carved shelves and decorations surrounding every wall. She sat in a plush chair, one of a few, and ran a hand over the tablecloth covering the desk. Only it wasn't really a desk. It was more like a dining table.

She felt so alone in that cabin. And she wondered what was happening to Captain Boswell.

CHAPTER THIRTY-FIVE

BENJAMIN MADISON MARCHED THE LENGTH of the *Vengeance Dragon*, his chin high and his hands clasped regally behind his back. Two sailors guarded the entrance to the pirate captain's cabin and they admitted him. Their expressions were stoic, yet their eyes were filled with the excitement of victory. Madison nodded to them as he entered.

Two of his men were dead and one was injured. The rest had sustained minor bruising. Madison had been told that Stephen Boswell had put up a good fight. But it hardly mattered now as Madison stood over his prisoner. The pirate had finally been defeated. He kneeled now, his hands bound, blood dripping from his lips. He looked much the same as Madison remembered. Despite the beating, he looked stronger, and underneath the blood and bruises on his face was weathered skin. This pirate life had no doubt changed him.

"Stephen Boswell," Madison said with a click of the tongue. "For eleven years I have hunted you, and here we are at long last."

"Lieutenant." The pirate's voice was a growl. Even now he dared to show defiance.

Madison snapped, "It's commodore now. I have risen through the ranks, gained power and command. And you? What have you become since last we met?"

"A captain."

Madison released a laugh full of mockery. "A captain of what? Dead men? You were nothing eleven years ago, and you are nothing now. I was right to judge you by your father's actions then. And now you will be hanged, just like him. I know that's what you fear and I am glad to know it. Justice will be done."

The commodore swelled with triumphant pride. It was short-lived when a man burst into the cabin. He gave a quick salute, touching the brim of his hat, and approached Madison to whisper in his ear.

"Alice Bradford is here. She's waiting in your cabin."

Madison felt his breath catch. Alice Bradford! He glanced at Boswell. The pirate was watching the floor.

"Put him under lock and key," Madison ordered. "Keep a guard on him. Some of his crew escaped. See if you can't get any names out of him. I'll be in my cabin."

He abruptly left, eager to see Alice, to make sure she was okay. He walked quickly, forcing himself not to break into a run to save some of his dignity. He pushed open the cabin door. Alice was sitting and she stood when he entered, turning around to look at him.

It was her. He had only seen her a few times, and the last had been a long time ago, but he knew it was her as soon as he laid eyes on her.

"Alice, do you recognize me?" he asked hurriedly, keenly.

She shook her head, but a smile was spreading across her face. She didn't need to recognize him to know who he was.

"It's me, Ben," he said all the same, and he squatted down and extended his arms and she ran into his embrace. She sobbed into his shoulder. He lifted her head, drying her tears with his thumbs, his own eyes sparkling. "I'm going to bring you home, Alice. Your mother is waiting for you. She never gave up hope." He gently asked, "Thomas? Your father?"

She shook her head, the smile fading.

"I'm sorry, Alice. But don't worry. You're safe now. We're going home." He hugged her again, thinking that this was a miracle, and trying to believe that it was Boswell who had been behind her disappearance this whole time.

An officer came to the door and Madison released Alice, straightening up. The officer held a stack of paper. He placed it on the table.

"Sir. The Articles were burned," he said. "This is the ship's log. We only skimmed it but saw no names. It seems Boswell only referred to his men by their position titles in everything he wrote. We've questioned him, but he hasn't given up anyone so far. We also asked that musician, Jerome Wistar, but he claims to have no information."

"Thank you."

Madison looked at Alice. She knew what he wanted to ask. She waited for him to ask it, an answer already prepared.

"Alice, can you tell me the names of any of the pirates who were on that ship?"

She shook her head. "No, I'm sorry. I don't know any."

He seemed to ponder her words, perhaps not quite believing them, but ultimately accepted them. Alice peered at the stack of paper. She froze. Captain Boswell's journal was stuck between some of the pages. While Ben gave the order to raise anchor, Alice quickly pulled it free and stuffed it into the waistline of her pants, pulling her shirt over to hide it. She breathed.

The ships moved out. The *Vengeance Dragon* went with them, manned by a crew of navy sailors. The pirate ship would be impounded once they returned to England, and then scrapped. It would take two months to cross the Atlantic and return to England. For most of the trip, Alice remained in the cabin. She spent time with Ben, catching up. And she spent time with Jerome. Ben didn't trust Jerome much, but he saw how close he and Alice had become during their time in captivity, and so he treated Jerome as much as a guest as he did Alice.

Alice couldn't stop thinking about Captain Boswell and how scared he must be. He was just below her, she knew, and at one point she asked Ben if she could see him.

"Why on earth would you want to see him?" Ben asked, and Alice shrugged, looking down. "I know you went through a lot, Alice, but you don't have to dwell on it. You're safe now and you don't have to see Boswell ever again."

Alice wasn't sure how to feel about that.

Eventually the English port neared. Jane Bradford waited there to greet her cousin, Ben, having no idea that her daughter was with him. The lead ship docked and the gangplank was put in place. Jane saw a little face peek over the bulwarks, heard a cry, and watched as Alice raced down the ramp. Jane dropped to her knees and received Alice into her arms. They clung to each other tightly, rocking back and forth, both sobbing.

Ben and Jerome approached and Jane stood, wiping her eyes with one hand and securing Alice to her side with another. She extended an arm toward Ben and he walked into her embrace.

"Thank you," she whispered before releasing him. She gave a curious glance at Jerome.

Ben cleared his throat. "This is Jerome Wistar, a musician. He was with Alice on the pirate ship."

They offered each other a quick greeting.

"Jane, there's something you should know." He lowered his voice, trying to soften it. "It was Stephen Boswell who had Alice. And we have him now."

Jane put a hand on her chest. She was at a loss for words. She tightened her grip on Alice. Eventually she cried, "What! How can that be?"

Ben touched her arm. "It's true, Jane. I'm sorry."

Jane shook her head. "I can't believe it."

A group of soldiers wearing red uniforms marched by in formation toward Ben's ship. One of higher rank stepped out of the group and addressed Ben when he was near enough.

"Commodore, congratulations on catching Stephen Boswell."

"Thank you. My men are waiting to give him to you."

The soldier gave a nod and then turned to Jane. "I am pleased to see you reunited with your daughter, Missus Bradford."

"Thank you."

He gave a small yet polite bow before following after his men.

"It's out of my hands now," Ben said. "Come, I'll walk you home."

"Can Jerome come with us?" Alice asked, looking up at her mother hopefully.

Jane examined Jerome. He was just a young man wearing poor bloke's clothing. He watched her with pleading eyes. But she could not invite him in, not like this. He was a stranger to her. There was already talk around town about her, about how she had refused to mourn over the disappearance of her husband and daughter, refused to accept that they were dead when everyone else had come to that conclusion. And then she had lived in that large house of hers, granted to her through Thomas' will, and turned down every suitor that came to her door.

Jerome seemed to catch on to her hesitation. "It's alright, I'll find somewhere to stay. An inn, maybe."

"But do you even have any money with you, Jerome?" Alice exclaimed.

Jane made a resolve. "Here." She dug around in her purse, pulling out a handful of high value coins. "Take this." And then she told him her address. "If you need anything, you're welcome to stop by."

"This is most irregular," Ben muttered.

"I don't care." Jane said, handing the coins over. "I mean it, Mister Wistar. If you need anything, anything at all, please come."

"Thank you very much," Jerome said, mustering all the sincerity he could. He smiled at Alice. "I'll visit, Alice."

Alice grinned at him. She waved as she departed with her mother and Ben. Jerome waited around for a bit. He knew the soldiers would be escorting Captain Boswell off the ship and to the prison soon, and he wanted to see him. The time came, and Jerome found he could only bear it for a few seconds.

The captain had been clapped in irons. We walked stiffly, surrounded on all sides by soldiers. He watched the ground and nothing else, his back hunched. He was a broken man.

Jerome turned away. He wished he hadn't seen that. He briskly left the port, started wandering toward the outskirts of town. Why had he let them take him to England? Why hadn't he asked to be brought to the colonies?

No, he didn't want to go to the colonies. There was nothing for him there. He would've been alone. His friends from the crew of the *Vengeance Dragon* were dead. Besides, he had wanted to stay with Alice. And she had been glad to have his company.

Jerome took another step. Someone grabbed him from behind, put a hand over his mouth. Jerome thrashed. Whoever had him forced him around a corner and then hissed in his ear, "Be still, will you!"

Jerome looked round. A huge grin swept across his face.

"Francis!" Then he punched his friend in the arm. "Why did you scare me like that?"

"Keep your voice down," Francis whispered. He quickly scanned the area. "Eight of us survived. We swam to shore. Reuben, Owen, and I convinced the others to come after

Captain Boswell. We stole a tiny ship, followed at a distance, and docked not far from here."

"What?" Jerome was elated. In fact, he tried not to laugh. "No one saw you? Wait, who's survived? What do you mean you're coming after Captain Boswell?"

"Would you shut up for just a moment?" Francis teased. "They don't know what we look like. They don't have our names." He hesitated. "Right?"

"Right!" Jerome said with pride.

Francis rolled his eyes. "Anyway, they also don't even know to look for us here. We just have to stay hidden until we come up with a plan. Titus, Reuben, Owen, Mather, Paisley, and two of those gents from the night watch are alive. Paisley isn't doing too good, though. He's bothered by what he did to Clinton."

Jerome shook his head, remembering when Clinton had tried to stop the mutiny singlehandedly, and Paisley had shot him, his own friend.

"But Jerome," Francis continued seriously. "I thought you'd like to help, and we could use you. We wouldn't expect you to fight, but you can help us plan. We're going to rescue Captain Boswell. Are you in?"

Jerome nodded.

CHAPTER THIRTY-SIX

THERE WAS A TRIAL, although to many it seemed a waste of time. The *Vengeance Dragon*'s log as well as the logs from the countless ships that Captain Boswell had attacked were enough evidence to convict him of piracy. And there had been enough witnesses present when he killed the commodore to charge him for that crime, as well. When asked if there was anything he would like to say in his defense, Captain Boswell remained silent. The judge sentenced him to hang by the neck until death.

The execution took place three days later. Alice remained at home, alone. Distraught, she curled up on the sofa in the sitting room, worrying her thumbs. She had wanted to attend, but Jane insisted she stay home.

Jane went to the gallows. She stood in the back of crowd, having arrived there later than everyone else. She wore black for her husband.

Captain Boswell, hands bound, was forced up the scaffold as the crowd jeered. His face was bruised and covered with dried blood and his steps were labored. Jane cringed at the sight. When the noose passed over his head, he suddenly became very frightened. He looked out beyond the people gathered before him but saw nothing, trapped in his own terrified thoughts. He was breathing hard and he appeared as though he might get sick at any moment, or even pass out.

And then the captain's eyes happened to wander to Jane and the two stared at each other. He gave her a look that was simply sadness. It broke her heart to see him this way, but she tried not to let it show. She had simply wanted to see him one last time, to try to remember the times they had spent together in their youth.

She wasn't reminded of that at all. All she could think was how he had changed into someone capable of killing her loved ones. Yet she clearly saw how scared he was now, how broken. Was this the same man she had known? He closed his eyes, and she never got an answer.

Benjamin Madison, standing off to the side, curled his lip when the executioner approached the lever. At long last it would be over. Justice would be done. Captain Boswell had his eyes shut tight, starting to panic as his sentence was read aloud to the crowd. To Jane, everything seemed to slow down. Then the lever was pulled and it all sped up.

The trap door Captain Boswell was standing on opened. The captain fell through. Madison smiled triumphantly. Jane turned away.

The rope around Captain Boswell's neck pulled taut. His eyes went wide. The crowd taunted as his body convulsed with writhes.

Someone broke through the crowd, pistols drawn, and fired at two soldiers. Other soldiers turned toward him, drawing their weapons. A second man emerged and fired two more shots at their backs. The crowd went into chaos, yelling and pushing to get away and mostly getting in the way of each other. A third man, taking cover from the confusion, sprinted up the scaffold and sliced the rope with a sword.

Captain Boswell plummeted to the ground. His legs took the impact, sending a shock through his body, and he toppled sideways. Four more men attacked the soldiers, springing on them from all sides. They each discharged two shots from two pistols and then engaged with swords. An eighth man ran to Captain Boswell's side, dashing off the noose around his neck and freeing his hands.

The sudden airflow into his lungs caused the captain to wheeze. He gasped and coughed, the veins in his neck protruding out.

"Just breathe, Stephen," Titus said to him, a hand on his shoulder. "Stephen, I'm so sorry. I'm so sorry."

Captain Boswell was unable to speak. All he could do was meet Titus' eye and shake his head.

"Let's get you out of here."

Titus helped Captain Boswell up and put his arms over his shoulders, supporting his weight. They ran as best they could like this, the other pirates following them protectively.

"Kill them!" Madison shouted frantically. "Don't let them get away!"

The soldiers weren't listening to him. Many of them had been killed or injured. One pirate remained in the area. He faced the last few soldiers who may have given chase to his comrades. He raised his sword, let out a yell, and ran at them, hacking like an animal, dropping them one by one. The battle cry died in his throat as they finally cut him down.

Madison picked up a gun that a soldier had dropped, ready to go after the pirates himself. But Jane, suddenly appearing at his side, put a hand on his arm to stop him.

"I have to go after them." His voice was wild.

"They'll kill you, Ben."

"Boswell needs to be caught and punished!"

"Don't you think he's been punished enough?"

Madison stared hard at Jane. Then he quickly looked away, angered by her words but not wanting her to know it. He glanced around the ground. Four of the pirates were dead. The rest had escaped with Boswell. No, wait. One was still alive. Madison stalked over to him. The man was choking on blood.

"Where did they go?" he demanded. The pirate smiled through his pain. It was unsettling. "Tell me!"

"You're too slow," he struggled to say. "I've outmaneuvered you once again."

"You're the helmsman?"

His smile grew. The title made him proud. Always had. He died, the smile frozen on his face.

The small band of pirates labored on, making their escape. Isaac Owen, Adam Paisley, and the two from the night watch were not with them. Paisley had made his last stand, ensuring their escape. As they reached the edge of the town they became reasonably sure they hadn't been followed and slowed a bit since both Captain Boswell and Reuben could not keep up the pace. Francis took the lead. Next came Titus, who still aided Captain Boswell, and Reuben. Mather brought up the rear, on constant alert for any threats.

They eventually came to a cliff surrounding an area of shore. A small ship was beached in the sand just below them. Jerome stood on its deck, waiting for them. They took their time traversing down the cliff. There was a meager path leading the way down and it would have been a relatively easy trek if not for both Captain Boswell and Reuben's inability to walk properly.

On board the ship, Titus brought Captain Boswell to the cabin. It was not furnished and there were no walls dividing it into more than one room, but there was a bed and Titus started to help Captain Boswell sit down on it.

Captain Boswell aggressively pulled away from Titus. He dropped onto the bed and glared at the other man.

"Just what had been going through your mind, Richard?" the captain growled, his voice hoarse and shaking. In fact, his whole body shook.

Titus crossed his arms defensively. "I just saved your life, Stephen."

"You nearly got me killed!"

"I didn't think the navy was going to attack us."

"You never think!" Captain Boswell shouted, and then he put a hand to his throat, wincing. The noose had chafed his skin raw. He lowered his voice. "You still haven't answered my question."

"I had to stop you," Titus said quietly. "No one else would've done it."

"Stop me?" The words dripped with sarcasm.

Titus dropped his act of innocence, took a step forward, and gave an outburst of his own. "You killed Addison!"

Captain Boswell would have stood if he could. He matched Titus' vehemence. "And you killed Paine!" He clenched a fist. "This was the worse-" His voice cracked and he didn't continue the sentence.

The two men glared at each other. Titus eventually softened and looked away, putting a hand to his forehead. "Stephen, at the time, you went too far. You put the crew at risk. I had to do something. I didn't mean for it to get out of hand."

Captain Boswell, still glaring angrily, had a comeback ready. He opened his mouth. Titus didn't give him the chance to speak.

"But in that last moment, when the British attacked, you could've jumped overboard like the rest of us and escaped. Reuben told me he saw you go into the cabin. And then Wistar told me that the Articles had been destroyed, that our names were safe. You were protecting us, even after what we did to you. I still think you crossed the line. But I was wrong to doubt your intentions. I shouldn't have acted so rashly. I should've talked to you, like you said." Titus took a deep breath, letting it out as he spoke. "And for that I'm sorry."

He chanced to look at the captain, expecting to still see fiery resentment. Instead there was only cautious deference. Captain Boswell took in Titus' words, and he hung his head, suddenly ashamed.

"You shouldn't have to apologize to me. I should apologize to you."

Titus plopped down next to his friend. "Let's leave it at that and move on."

Captain Boswell agreed gratefully. Then they sat in silence for a while.

The captain cast a sideways glance at Titus. "How did you know who Alice was?"

"Her mannerisms always reminded me of Jane. And I could see the resemblance," he said. "And then she recognized Lieutenant Madison's name and I pieced it together."

"It's commodore now," Captain Boswell muttered with annoyance. "Still, I never saw Jane in her. I feel like a fool now."

Titus said quickly and quietly, "Well, in our youth, I was jealous of you and her."

"Jealous?" Captain Boswell shifted to face Titus.

Titus put his elbows on his knees and his hands on his cheeks, embarrassed. "Yes. Jane talked to me about you once. About how she felt sorry for you. And I became jealous, because I loved her." He shook his head. "Stephen, I think you should talk to her."

Captain Boswell snorted. "What makes you think she would want to see me?"

"Because she loved you." Titus met his eye. "She told me so herself. She came to me once. Said she was confused. She was eager to get married, but part of her felt like she was letting you down."

Captain Boswell was stunned into silence. Slowly, slowly, he nodded. "I need to meet with her. She must think so low of me. I need to explain myself." But then he tensed as he remembered seeing her at the execution. "She was there, Richard. At the gallows. She was there. What if she doesn't want to see me?"

"You might as well try. You have a second chance." Titus stood. "Wistar knows her address. I'll send him in."

And Jerome entered the cabin after being beckoned by Titus. He smiled at Captain Boswell, relieved to see him recovering.

"What can I do for you, sir?"

"I need you to relay a message to Jane Bradford."

CHAPTER THIRTY-SEVEN

ALICE HADN'T KNOWN HOW TO FEEL BEFORE. But she knew now. When Ben and her mother gave her the news that Captain Boswell had escaped and was alive, she grinned from ear to ear, relieved to hear it. She couldn't hide her delight.

"What's the matter with you?" Ben said, bothered. "Why are you smiling?"

"Because he's alive!"

Ben shook his head and moved into the sitting room, collapsing onto a sofa. "Have you forgotten what he's done? All that time on his ship, I presume you saw him do a lot of terrible things."

"All that time on his ship gave me time to think."

Jane put a hand on her daughter's shoulder. "Hush, Alice."

Alice met her mother's eyes. "But Mother, surely you are happy that he's alive. He's your friend."

"He *was* my friend," Jane clarified. "He's changed. I don't know who he is anymore."

"He's the same!" Alice claimed. "Was he not quiet and fearful when he was younger? Well, he still is now. And he cares. He cared about his crew. He cared about me."

"No he didn't," Ben spat. "Really, what's gotten into you? I believe your mind has been manipulated. You were his captive. He killed your grandfather. He killed your father."

"Ben," Jane snapped, feeling that he was going too far. He seemed to catch himself, remembering that he was speaking to a child.

He stood up suddenly. "I am wasted here. I need to find him."

Jane sighed. "You don't even know where to look."

"It took me eleven years to get this far. *Eleven years.* I'm not going to let him slip away this time."

He let himself out. Jane sat Alice down next to her and stroked her hair.

"Alice, there's a lot you don't understand."

"You think he's changed, fine. He can change again," Alice insisted. "The fact that I'm here proves it. He protected me. The last time you saw him was eleven years ago. Now you only know what you've heard. But I've been with him for all these months. I've seen so much. He's done terrible, terrible things. But he's capable of doing good things. He's just gotten lost. You need to give him a chance."

"And the crimes he's committed? The lives he's taken… from our own family?" Jane pressed. "Does it all mean nothing?"

"I never said that. Just that you need to give him a chance."

Someone knocked on the door and they both jumped, engrossed in their conversation. Jane got up and tentatively approached the door, not expecting anyone to drop by. When she saw that it was Jerome Wistar, she opened it. She never got a chance to greet him, or to voice her surprise at seeing him so soon, or to inquire if he had heard the news about Captain Boswell's escape.

"Missus Bradford, I have a message," he said quickly. "It's from Captain Boswell and I beg of you to hear it out." He never even gave her a chance to respond. He simply kept talking. "The captain knows you may not wish to see him, and he knows his actions may be inexcusable, but he would like to offer you an explanation. Not to make excuses, but so that you may understand. He'd like to meet with you. Tomorrow morning I can come back and bring you to him. All he's asking for is a chance."

Jane looked back at Alice. Her daughter was smiling and nodding her head. Torn, Jane wasn't sure if this was the right thing to do, but she hesitantly relented. Jerome thanked her profusely and then ran off to tell the captain.

Benjamin Madison walked away from the Bradford house. He had been standing just around the corner, out of sight but not out of earshot. Now he needed to prepare for tomorrow morning.

CHAPTER THIRTY-EIGHT

JEROME BROUGHT JANE AND ALICE to the beach where the pirates were hiding out. Captain Boswell waited for them nervously. Alice was proud to see that his rapier was once again at his side. And so was Titus. Looking up at the ship, she saw three familiar faces peering down from over the bulwarks; Reuben, Francis, and Mather. She waved up at them and they waved back. Jane glanced at her, astounded and frightened at their friendliness to her.

Once they had approached, Titus and Jerome joined the others on the ship. Captain Boswell and Jane looked at each other in silence. The bruises covering him looked so painful. He had turned up his collar to hide the scar around his neck from the noose. But Jane could see some of it, right in the front where the collar split and exposed some skin.

Alice was the first to speak. "I'm glad you're okay," she said. He let his gaze shift down to her, the ghost of a smile touching his lips.

"As am I about you, Alice."

He looked to Jane once again.

"Stephen." It was the only greeting she could give.

"Jane." His voice was quiet.

"I never expected to see you again."

Captain Boswell glanced down and then up. He cleared his throat, gestured down the beach. "Let's take a walk."

He led the way. His steps were heavy, but that was the only sign he gave of his injuries. Jane walked next to him, although she put quite a distance between them, and she held onto Alice's hand. Jane watched him the whole time, and he watched the ground that he walked over.

"I couldn't believe it when Ben told me you were behind Alice's disappearance," she said. "After all this time, for you to suddenly show up again, is unimaginable."

"I never meant to hurt you, Jane."

"No?" She didn't bother hiding her incredulity. "You shot my father, Stephen. You hadn't been aiming at him, but when you saw him, you shot him. That sounds rather deliberate to me."

He abruptly stopped walking, finally looking at her. They had gone quite a distance from the ship. "I was scared. I was in pain. All I saw was the commodore. I didn't see him as your father. I just wanted to get out of there."

"Fine," she snapped, making clear that she didn't really think so. "So then what? You became a pirate and went on a murdering rampage because, why, exactly?"

"I didn't…." He cut himself off, glancing about as if the right words might appear in front of him. What he said next came out harshly. "I was afraid, Jane. I thought I could protect myself by killing."

Jane shook her head. "You know, I understand that you had a hard time in the navy. I get that my father may not have been the kindest to you. I knew very well who your father was. But I befriended you all the same. I thought you could be better than your father. But then you became him, and you took my father from me. And then you took my husband."

Alice shook her hand out of her mother's. "But he didn't take me! He brought me home."

Captain Boswell put a hand out in a negative gesture, and shook his head. "Alice."

Jane took her daughter's hand again. "I'm sure that hadn't been your intent."

"You're right," the captain admitted, though there was no emotion in his voice.

"Do you expect me to forgive you? Is that what you want?"

"No. I would never ask that of you."

"So you got your revenge as a pirate and now you want redemption?" Jane's voice rose, anger creeping into it.

"No."

"Then what, Stephen? Why did you ask me here?"

"Acceptance."

For a moment all they heard was the rush of water flowing steadily onto the beach, and then receding with each new wave.

Captain Boswell breathed in a lungful of the salty air. "You spoke to me when no one else would. You listened when no one else would. Jane, you accepted me then. I can be that person again."

Jane searched his eyes carefully. At last she said, "I don't think of you like that anymore. I've moved on."

"I don't care how you think of me." Captain Boswell put a hand to his eyes briefly, rethinking his words. "I mean, that's not what I'm interested in. When we're done talking here, my men and I are going to get on that ship and sail far away. We'll go into hiding. I don't know where. But wherever we end up, Jane, I want to know that you can see past what I've become, and can still accept me for who I was. Because you matter to me. As does what you think of me. And I don't want my actions, no matter how unforgivable, to ruin our past."

Another silence. Jane could see the plea in his eyes. Those icy, dark blue, familiar eyes. Alice looked at her also, with the same plea written across her bright, sky blue eyes. Jane swept back her daughter's hair tenderly.

"What do you think about this, Alice?"

"You know what I think, Mother."

Jane hesitated visibly. She didn't speak for an eternity, thinking. At last she told him, in a voice lined with cold, "I can move on from the past if that's what you want, but I can't forget it. Can you live with that?"

Captain Boswell gave a nod.

"And you need to remember that I loved Thomas as much as I cared for you."

Another nod.

A pause from Jane. "Then I'll give you this chance, and the acceptance you seek."

He closed his eyes and thanked her, his relief evident. All of a sudden she felt like she might cry. What she had just done, she realized, had been just as important for her as it had been for him. He was such a sad, broken man, and she couldn't bear to see him like that. She felt that she should say something more, anything.

Commodore Madison never gave her the opportunity. He stepped away from the base of the cliff, having just climbed down, and approached Captain Boswell, aiming a pistol in each hand. Jane, surprised, drew Alice away several paces.

The commodore extended his arms out. "This ends now." He let both pistols drop by his side. And he drew a rapier. He pointed it at Captain Boswell while putting himself into the en-garde stance and digging his feet into the sand. "Let's see how much you've improved since the last time we crossed blades."

Captain Boswell said nothing. He drew his sword, his face set in malicious concentration. He never hesitated. He attacked first.

CHAPTER THIRTY-NINE

THE TWO SWORDSMEN STEPPED back and forth, striking and parrying repeatedly, their blades dancing. Commodore Madison's form was beautiful, his motions fluid. Captain Boswell's movements looked forced as he lacked proper form, yet he fought with an aggression that Commodore Madison had no choice but to be wary of.

"Mother, can't you do something?" Alice asked.

Worry lines creased Jane's forehead. "I can't stop this. It's what they both want." She feared for both men.

Captain Boswell's injuries painfully flared up in protest to all this movement. Yet the captain gritted his teeth and pushed through it. His legs, ribs, chest, all screamed at him. He focused on the commodore, on his arrogance, on the torment he had caused him, and he let it drive him.

Commodore Madison knew where his enemy was hurt the most, and he tried to press forward on those sore spots. He tried to take advantage of the captain's slowness in his legs, stepping in quick and hard. Yet the captain's sword arm was just as quick and he always managed to block each strike.

They both saw the face of a villain.

On the next block, Commodore Madison used his left arm to tangle up Captain's Boswell sword. Blood spurted. He pressed down on his sword and pushed his weight into the captain, driving his sword point into the captain's thigh. Both men let out a groan of pain. Then the commodore tried to bend the captain's sword away. As his chest became undefended, Captain Boswell kicked up sand into the commodore's face. He followed the commodore's backward jerk with a lunge, ignoring the intensified agony in his legs, and penetrated the commodore's shoulder.

The commodore grabbed Captain Boswell's sword arm with his free hand to keep him from retreating after the lunge. He brought his own sword around and tried to stab his enemy square in the chest. The captain pivoted and grasped the blade coming at him with his bare hand, his palm becoming smeared with blood.

The two men grappled with each other like this, all form abandoned, each straining against the other. Captain Boswell twisted his sword arm and brought his elbow down sharply, breaking the commodore's grip. Then he brought his sword hilt across his body to punch the commodore's right arm, weakening it. He stepped in and rotated toward the blade while wrapping an arm around the other man's sword and pulling, effectively disarming his enemy.

Yet even as Commodore Madison lost his weapon, he attacked the captain with his fists and managed to get in a couple of powerful blows. Captain Boswell, unable to follow up his disarming move, stumbled. The commodore saw his opening. He rushed the captain. The captain got low, ready to take the impact and reciprocate it. They collided into each other, and both fell backward away from each other, sprawling into the sand.

Each man was dazed. Captain Boswell opened and closed his eyes, trying to clear the stars that had invaded his vision. He drew strength from his rapier, still in his hand. He pushed himself up, first onto his knees, and then onto one foot.

Commodore Madison shook his head to clear it. He felt in the sand for his sword, hoping that Captain Boswell had also let go of his during the fall. He felt metal. But it was no sword. It was a gun. He didn't bother standing. He lifted himself with one arm, leaning on it to turn around, and swung the pistol out toward Captain Boswell with his other arm.

Captain Boswell regained his feet. He turned. And that's when the shot was fired.

The bullet hit him in the stomach. He let out a breath. He felt that he had been punched by a large mass. He staggered back, trying to stay on his feet. With a cry he sank to his knees, dropping his sword, his hands in the sand.

Titus heard the shot from the ship. He didn't use the gangplank. He just vaulted over the side, landed in a few inches of water, and broke into a run.

Commodore Madison tossed the gun aside. He picked up the other, a couple of feet away, and stood. He calmly stepped toward the captain. Alice tried to run over there, to do what, she wasn't sure, but Jane held her back, knowing too well that it could be dangerous to interfere.

Captain Boswell held his hands to the gunshot wound. As he raised his head to look at Commodore Madison, the commodore brought his pistol level to the captain's head. He tightened his finger on the trigger.

"No!" Alice shrieked.

Titus dove and tackled Commodore Madison. He had both hands on the commodore, one on his arm, trying to push it down, and the commodore strained to keep his gun pointed at Captain Boswell's head. He fired as they fell.

They hit the ground and looked to see where the bullet had landed, one with eagerness and the other with dread, both holding their breath.

Captain Boswell was forced onto his back by the bullet, a fresh red stain spreading across his chest.

Alice broke from Jane and ran to the captain's side. She clutched his arm. Titus rolled on top of Commodore Madison, grabbed a fistful of the front of his shirt, and punched him in the nose with not enough force to knock him out, but enough to keep him down for now. Then he joined Alice.

There was blood in the captain's mouth. He gasped, but he could get no air. His whole body burned. He clenched a hand, the pain too much.

"Just hold on, Stephen," Titus said. His voice shook. Alice sobbed next to him.

Jane approached. She knelt down. Put a hand on Captain Boswell's shoulder. "Stephen," she said gently. "Look at me. Just look at me."

He obeyed, letting his eyes focus on her face. The rest of the world was out of focus. The edges of his sight were fading, turning to black. He was so scared. He didn't want to die. He didn't want to die.

Jane slipped her hand into his. She leaned forward. Whispered in his ear. Touched her lips to his forehead. His face was wet with tears. He didn't want to die. He didn't want to die.

She pulled away. Still, he stared at her. Yet his eyes had lost their light. His eyes had lost their life. She closed them. He was dead.

Titus stood. Reuben, Mather, Francis, and Jerome were there. No words passed between them. No words were needed. Commodore Madison sat up. Titus drew his cutlass and stomped toward him, a low growl escaping him. The commodore tried to hurry to his feet but Titus was already there.

"Stop." Alice's voice was sharp. Titus froze. "Don't hurt him. He's family."

Titus backed down, but not before giving Commodore Madison a threatening glare. The commodore stared at Alice and Titus, aghast.

"You command these pirates?"

"No," she said. "No one commands them. But they respect me and I respect them."

CHAPTER FOURTY

THEY BURIED HIM ON THAT BEACH, close to the water so the high tide would keep him hidden. They buried him with his sword. The grave was left unmarked. The pirates stood around it, their heads bowed. They were silent, save sniffling from Jerome. Titus remained down on one knee, and Reuben kept a hand on his shoulder. The older man occasionally wiped his eyes.

Commodore Madison stood with Jane and Alice. Jane leaned into him.

"You will not tell a soul where his body is, Benjamin," she told him.

"I am a commodore. It is expected of me that I find him and deliver him, dead or alive."

"Then perhaps you should step down." She kept her voice even. Neutral.

Then it was time for the pirates to leave. They took turns touching their captain's grave before walking away from it. Alice said goodbye to each one of them. Reuben hugged her tight.

"Thank you for everything, Mister Reuben," she said.

"You'll do good things, little lady," he replied.

Titus shook Jane's hand. She smiled at the gesture.

Jerome was staying behind. He was no pirate. He deserved better, the others had decided. Jane offered to hire him. He could help with the business and stay at their home, opinions of others be damned.

Mather shook his hand. Francis gave him a full sack of coins. "Buy a new fiddle and never stop playing."

The four pirates got on their ship. They sailed away, no destination in mind.

Benjamin Madison walked Jane, Alice, and Jerome home. He would resign from his position, making public his inability to recapture Boswell. No one would know that the pirate captain had already been killed. No one but eight.

When she was alone, Alice retrieved the captain's journal. She knew she needed to destroy it, but for now she couldn't bring herself to do it. She flipped through the pages haphazardly, simply needing to hold something of his. If not for that need, she would not have remembered that there was still an entry she had not read. She flipped to the back where it started.

And she read the last words of Captain Stephen Boswell.

CHAPTER FOURTY-ONE

~ 1727, Fall ~

I MET ALICE BRADFORD THREE MONTHS AGO. She boarded my ship and in doing so her life was saved.

I remember it more clearly than I do most other events I have seen. She cowered behind some crates, afraid. That look of fear was not new to me. Nor was fear coupled with courage. Alice certainly had courage. She put on a brave face despite the tears. But she was so young. So young.

I wanted to talk with her, and that was all. I was interested in learning about her and understanding her. But I suppose that interest was where the rest of it all stemmed from. Isn't it?

I was going to kill her. I didn't know when, but I was as certain as I always have been about everyone else that I have ever killed. Why did I even keep her alive as long as I did before finally deciding to do it? What made me wait?

The day we attacked the Spanish trader shortly after the *Sea Maiden* itself was the day I made up my mind. After the attack when I saw Alice run from the deck to the cabin, realizing that she had seen the entire encounter, I knew I was going to do it right then and there. I drew my sword as I went to her. Yet I felt I needed to speak to her first or it wouldn't be right. Even that wasn't like me. And I don't know what happened after I did. She talked back to me, not in her own defense, but to antagonize me. And somehow her words stayed my blade, although I'm certain she had had no idea of my intentions or how close to death she had been. She angered me, and in doing so she saved her own life. Again.

So many days had already gone by. In all that time I hadn't even pursued my original intent to understand her. What was I thinking? What was I hoping to accomplish?

She tried to escape. She didn't realize the dangers. I had just dealt with Reed and was walking back to the ship with Richard when something made me turn down a different road. Richard followed me, although I could tell he was confused. And then I saw Alice being accosted. I don't know what came over me. I just ran in and attacked that man, suddenly so angry at him for hurting her. I took a beating for her.

When she became ill, I felt so hopeless. Like I was lost. How did she have that effect on me? Reuben saved her life. He spoke with me, and I realized then that I wasn't going to kill her. Not anymore. How could I? And thinking back now, having spent all this time with her, it pains me to know that I had ever thought about ending her life at all.

She's only ten years old. I still can't believe it. She has said things to me, amazing things. She has seen the worst of me. She has seen what I'm capable of. Yet over time, she has come to care, as if she sees me as a human being. She still looks at me sometimes with fear and sometimes with horror. She looks at me the way I've seen countless people look at me as they watch me destroy their lives. Yet there is also concern in her eyes. And I can't help but wonder if that concern is genuine, or if her being here has manipulated her young mind.

What am I supposed to do now? Keep her on my ship forever? She's just a child. I have to remind myself of that sometimes. I can't bring her home. I can't let her go. But I think I fear for her.

I'd like to hope that someday she will be free. But I suppose the only way that would happen is if I'm killed or caught, and I will never let that happen. And one day I'd like to be free of the British for good. I can't know the future. But it'd be nice to think that way, that we could both get our freedom.

I'm glad I met her. I'm glad she came into my life. I want her to know that I didn't mean for any of this to happen. If I could do right by her, I would, but it's impossible now. I won't do anything that would risk my life. That's why I need to kill at all. I wish she could understand that. I wish I had the courage to explain it to her, to tell her about everything I've been through. I still think about all that…

Still, I can protect her, as I have been doing. I'll always protect her. She matters to me, I think. And I never thought I would feel this way. If I could have anything from her, it would be her acceptance of me. Genuine acceptance. And maybe it wouldn't be a stretch to think I already have it. Would that be wrong, after what I've done to her? Maybe I don't deserve it. But I can still hope. Can't I?

ABOUT THE AUTHOR

JULIA MAIOLA is a professional ice cream scooper from Rochester, New York. She will receive her Bachelor's in English at the end of 2018 and will continue to develop her writing. THE RED FLAG is her first novel, the first of many to come. A science fiction title is currently in the works and will be followed by more in the fantasy and historical fiction genres. When Julia is not writing, she is gaming and skateboarding, but most of her spare time is spent reading adventure novels.